Alan Gibbons

In addition to being a popular and prolific writer for children, Alan Gibbons teaches in a primary school. He is also much in demand as a speaker in schools and at book events. He lives in Liverpool with his wife and four children.

Alan Gibbons has twice been shortlisted for the Carnegie Medal, with *The Edge* and *Shadow of the Minotaur*, which also won the Blue Peter Book Award in the 'Book I Couldn't Put Down' category.

THE LEGENDEER TRILOGY

Shadow of the Minotaur
Vampyr Legion
Warriors of the Raven

THE TOTAL FOOTBALL SERIES

Some You Win . . .
Injury Time
Last Man Standing
Twin Strikers
Final Countdown

Caught in the Crossfire
Chicken
Dagger in the Sky
The Dark Beneath
The Edge
Ganging Up
Julie and Me . . . and Michael Owen Makes Three
Julie and Me : Treble Trouble
Not Yeti
Playing with Fire
Whose Side Are You On?

THE LOST BOYS' APPRECIATION SOCIETY

ALAN GIBBONS

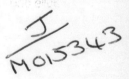

A Dolphin
Paperback

First published in Great Britain in 2004
as a Dolphin paperback
by Orion Children's Books
a division of the Orion Publishing Group Ltd
Orion House
5 Upper St Martin's Lane
London WC2H 9EA

A catalogue record for this book
is available from the British Library

Typeset at The Spartan Press Ltd,
Lymington, Hants

Printed and bound in Great Britain by
Clays Ltd, St Ives plc

ISBN 1 84255 095 0

BEFORE

There was no premonition, no hint of danger round the corner. Death waited expectantly, hunched in shadows.

Lisa Cain was on the way home from a pleasant afternoon spent in the company of Marie, an old schoolfriend. She was driving sensibly as usual, over-cautiously according to the driver of the racing-green Rover that had been impatiently tailgating her for the five minutes before the crash.

'But it had been raining heavily,' he told police later, maybe that explained it.

She did speed up, moments before the crash, most probably intimidated by the closeness of the Rover. She did it against her own better judgement, but she did it. She pressed her foot down on the accelerator.

Coming in the opposite direction, Steve Parsons was also on his way home from a day with friends. He'd been drinking, he admitted that, but he could hold his alcohol. Everybody said that about Steve. He didn't like to boast but he had been known to put ten pints away and still drive home safely. Lisa Cain knew nothing about Steve Parsons until he entered her life at 4:17 p.m. that winter's afternoon, coming round the bend on the wrong side of the road. He was doing seventy but, Hell, he was a good driver!

Lisa's stomach clenched in horror. She braked hard, but the Rover behind was too close. It clipped the back of her car sending her into a deadly spin. Almost simultaneously striking the wing of Steve Parsons' Toyota, Lisa Cain careered through a hedge. The steering wheel was jolted from her hands. Her car bumped through a gate and into a field. The last thing she saw was the tree trunk. Lisa Cain's breath burst from her as her car slammed into the sturdy oak. Her life ended there.

It started with a phone call. Quite how long it had been ringing before I heard it I'm not sure. The house was bedlam that afternoon, all Gary's fault of course. He had just been flicking cold baked beans at me and skipped out of reach as I took a swipe at him.

Dr-ing.

I jerked to attention. I seemed to understand right away that the call was urgent. I went to get up from the table but Gary started calling me names so I took another swipe at him.

Dr-ing.

Somehow the tone seemed more insistent, almost shrill.

'Give over,' I said. 'Can't you hear the phone ringing?'

Gary could hear all right but he didn't care. That's the way it is with Gary, he never knows when to stop. He thinks he's Jack the lad, a real funny guy. The truth is, he's training to be the world's greatest pillock. In fact, it's the only thing he puts any effort into, his pillockness. He flicked another cold, congealed lump of beany gunge in my direction, spattering my new Ellesse top. It had been flawlessly cream and cool until Gary got to work on it. That did it. I finally flipped and sprang at him. I was coming round the corner of the table when I met resistance. My legs suddenly stiffened and stopped working. Before I could do a thing about it I stumbled, pitched forward and fell flat on my face. Gary had tied my shoelaces together without me noticing! How does he do that? I didn't feel a thing.

'How old *are* you?' I yelled as I rolled over onto my back. 'That's a stupid kid's trick.'

Dr-ing!

The prolonged ringing was beginning to worry me. Whoever was on the other end wasn't giving up. They were determined to get an answer. Desperate – and in my mind desperation equals importance.

'Gary, will you get that!'

He just laughed. The spectacle of me rolling about like an upturned beetle was clearly far more entertaining than something as mundane as answering the phone. I was still trying to unknot my laces when Dad came stamping downstairs. I heard him pick up the handset.

'Didn't either of you hear it?' he grumbled. 'I was up in the loft trying to find your mum's sewing machine before she gets home. You'd think you could do one little thing for me.'

'I heard it,' I snapped, 'but El Divvo here tied my shoelaces together.'

Dad was still barking at us when somebody spoke at the other end.

'You behave yourself, Gary,' said Dad. 'No arguments.'

Gary tried to come back with a smart riposte. He has an answer for everything, our Gary. But Dad wasn't in the mood.

'Just shut it!' he yelled.

The caller must have objected at that point because Dad immediately said, 'No, not you.'

There was a moment's hesitation, then a sound like something bursting, imploding, but far away, as though somebody had pulled the plug on the day. I finally undid my laces and walked to the door. It was for all the world as if the air had been completely sucked out of the hallway. Something was wrong. The anger-flash had drained out of Dad's face, replaced by a blank pallor.

Like disbelief—

Like horror—

'Say—that—again.'

His voice trailed away into the half-light, the final word disintegrating into the dusk. Gary had joined me in the doorway. He too had heard the implosion, a sound beyond hearing almost, a resonance that shuddered through the house, pulling down certainties, ripping apart normalities. I was looking at Dad, trying to make eye contact, but he continued to stare ahead.

'Dad?'

He held up his hand. His Adam's apple was working strangely in his throat as if he were choking noiselessly. I remembered what he had been doing in the loft – looking for Mum's sewing machine.

Hers.

My mum's.

The link was made in my mind. Suddenly, as if it had been whispered into my ear by some evil spirit, I knew exactly what the call was about. I questioned Dad with my eyes but still he wouldn't return the look. I was making a silent plea, begging it not to be bad news, begging it not to be her. Then I watched Dad's hand go to his face and cover his mouth. Time stood still as his eyes shut tight, squeezing away the threatening tears. He refused to let them come. Even then, even at that moment when our lives broke apart, he continued to play the game. Big boys don't cry.

* * *

I don't remember much about the rest of that day. I remember that Gary and I sat in front of the TV. We didn't watch it. We were too broken, too torn up inside for that.

Instead, we kind of stared through the screen, trying to make sense of the shifting images, trying to come to terms with what had just happened. Meanwhile, Dad crashed around the house, shouting from time to time, not about

6

anything in particular, you understand, just shouting, letting out the despair. I think he was beginning to understand what life would be like without her. He worked, of course, but Mum did everything else. She did the planning and took the decisions, then let Dad think they'd come up with them together.

Then, a few hours later, my grandparents were with us while Dad went—

Crazy, isn't it? It's now only eleven months later, not even a year, but I still don't know where he went that day. To the hospital, I suppose. I don't know the score – how soon they let you see someone who is dying, and I dare say I'll never ask him. I don't think I could find the words.

Eventually, Gary spoke. Grandad was on the phone. Grandma was making us a meal we would never eat. So we were alone in the late afternoon gloom, with the amber streetlights blurring into the living room.

And this is what Gary said: 'I was acting the fool.'

'What?'

'Mum was dying and I was acting the fool.'

Then I had the same picture, the two of us wrestling round like a pair of prize idiots while Mum lay broken against the steering wheel. Gary and I, we're as different as two brothers can be. I'm the swot, the whizz-kid, the Poindexter. I didn't choose to be. I just am. Gary, he's your prototype scally, all practical jokes and lost homework. But in that moment we were united in one thing, a feeling of guilt so strong the day shrank to a brilliant white point then died suddenly.

* * *

Days later. Was it days? I don't know. Maybe it was weeks. The mind plays tricks on you, doesn't it? It sucks you into a tunnel where memory goes shaky and unreliable, lost in the wind-roar of pain and hurt and don't-let-it-be-true.

7

Days later, yes, I'm sure it was days, we were sitting in church, heads bowed. There were red roses everywhere, her flowers. They played Mum's favourite songs: *The Story of the Blues* and *Heart as Big as Liverpool*, music that was like her. Then Pete Wylie, the lead singer, sang this one line:

'*And I am not alone.*'

I crumpled, trying to fight back the tears. I suppose it was true in one way. We weren't alone. We had each other. We were surrounded by the wider family: uncles, aunts, cousins, grandparents. Plus, I had a purpose, always had. I wanted Mum back. Of course I did. I needed her still. But she'd shown me how to make my own way. She'd given me that strength.

But for Dad and Gary, each in their own way, I think it was even worse. They depended on Mum so much. While she'd taught me to pretty much stand on my own feet, get on with my studies, find myself in the books we both loved, the pair of them were useless without her. Dad, for starters, whenever she was away, even for a day, he was like a big, dumb puppy trailing round the house, pining. How was he going to cope now?

As for Gary, it was even worse. He lived for the moment, but suddenly every moment was empty. In the days after her death, he couldn't find anyone else who really mattered. He *was* alone. Desperately so, crushed by loneliness. One evening the three of us were sitting, not speaking, in the kitchen. The dusk had gathered round us but nobody had got up to switch on the light. Nobody cared enough to move. The radio was on though, an old Hollies hit from the Sixties: *He Ain't Heavy, He's My Brother*.

Funny thing about music, the way it seems to hang in the air, a web of half-forgotten tunes waiting their time, then it speaks your thoughts for you. Anyway, I looked at Gary

8

and made my decision: however much I was hurting I was going to swallow it down and be there for Gary. He needed me.

At the funeral, we were standing huddled in the rain while the vicar did his earth-to-earth, ashes-to-ashes stuff. We each dropped a single red rose on the coffin but Gary's hand shook so much his flower missed and he had to do it again. We were saying goodbye to Mum, giving her up, watching her slide into the ground. I watched Gary, knowing he was taking it the hardest, slowly crumbling inside. I was going to be there for him, but it wasn't going to be easy. I saw the light go out in his eyes. I saw the night come.

* * *

I think we had started to lose Gary even before Mum died, while she was lying between life and death at the hospital. The doctor had told us not to get our hopes up. He told us that, even if Mum came to, or by some miracle actually managed to speak to us, there was little hope. Her injuries were just too severe. The crash had broken her up inside. In real terms, she had died when she hit the tree. But Gary hoped. When he saw Mum's eyes open he thought, he *knew*, that she was coming back to us.

'My boys,' she said weakly, in a voice that seemed to float up from somewhere outside her. 'My lost boys.'

Then she closed her eyes and a scream shuddered through Gary. Only it wasn't a real scream. It was silent. He was gagging on his own pain.

* * *

Months later, and this time I'm certain it was months, we got dressed up in our best clothes. It was the first time we'd had them on since the funeral. For our day in court, Dad said, for our portion of justice. But we didn't get justice.

9

What we got was an insult. The driver was over the limit, three times over. He'd been drinking all day. He had some cock and bull line about pressure of work but it was all crocodile tears. What's disgusting is: it worked. He walked. Do you know what he got? A suspended sentence!

That's right, he rips the heart out of our family and he walks away with a lousy suspended sentence. The last I saw of him he was hugging his own family and thanking his solicitor.

For Dad and me it was a kick in the teeth. But for Gary it was the end. He'd always been that kind of kid: on edge, fragile. Mum and Dad always used to say how different we were, even as babies. I'd sleep the day away while Gary would be up all hours screaming the house down. I was placid and hard-working at school while Gary was bored and distracted.

We played this game sometimes, choosing a spirit for each one of us, a creature that summed up our personality. Dad was a bear, grumpy but basically comfortable to be with. Mum was a dolphin, free, joyous, a true rescuer of souls. I was a dog, faithful and loyal. Gary was a monkey of course, tetchy, restless and full of mischief.

Funny thing, even though Gary always liked to think of himself as streetwise and tough, he was always the closest to her, the mummy's boy. So long as she was there, the dolphin would always be on hand when the monkey fell from his tree. But she died and he found out that there was no justice in the world. And all that he had of her, all that was left of his childhood were her last words:

'My boys, my lost boys.'

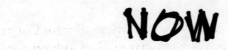

NOW

1

Dad is struggling with his tie, the new silk one, all purple and shiny with embossed black stripes. It's a real tussle and the tie is winning.

'Going out?' I ask.

I seem to remember he told me something this morning, but I was too busy packing my school bag to pay much attention.

'Yes, that's OK, isn't it?'

'Dad,' I say. 'You don't need my permission to go out.'

But he seems to think he does, which makes me understand. It's a date, his first since Mum died. Tension crackles round us. It's eleven months since the crash but nobody's anywhere near moving on. We're frozen in a teardrop of time. The truth is, we've only taken half a step back from the graveside. The three of us are standing still, that's all, muddling along waiting for life to start again. What do I think of Dad seeing somebody new? I don't know. The way life is at the moment, we're all making up the rules as we go along. I watch Dad grunting and snarling at the tie. He wants to look his best but with his hands – great spades of things – there's no chance. If Dad's genetically engineered to do anything, it is to erect scaffolding.

'Maybe I do need your permission,' Dad says, flipping listlessly at the deformed tangle that is his attempt at a tie-knot. 'You think it's too early to be seeing someone, don't you?'

'Dad,' I say, wishing he hadn't asked. 'That's for you to decide.'

He nods.

'I don't even know her that well. She works in the offices.'

'Secretary?'

'Typist, word-processor, whatever they call them these days.'

'And you like her?'

'Dunno,' he says. 'That must be what I'm trying to find out.'

He pinches the bridge of his nose.

'Jeez,' he says. 'Do you think I'm making a mistake?'

Not only is it eleven months since Mum died, it is also eighteen years since Dad last went out on a date, and it shows. When his idea of romance for well over a decade had been doing the gardening together, and when a night out was a movie followed by a Chinese banquet, I suppose you could say he's forgotten the A-Z of courtship. Not that I can imagine Dad ever getting beyond D in the alphabet of love. He and Mum were childhood sweethearts. They met at school, decided to get engaged on the Mersey Ferry, got married at nineteen, had me when they were twenty-one. That's pretty much it. Eighteen months later Gary came along and then Dad had the snip. Two lads, as he never tires of telling us, is enough for anybody.

Look at him. There's this vein in his temple that keeps throbbing like a worm turning soil and I can actually hear his teeth grinding. He does that when he's nervous. It's a wonder he's got any enamel left at all.

'Do you realise,' Dad says, 'I've hardly been out of the house in the evening since your mum went? I tried going to the pub a few weeks back, but I only lasted one pint. I went everywhere with Lisa. She's what made me tick. I don't know how to do things on my own any more.'

14

'Is that why you fixed up this date?'

Dad sighs.

'I need to do something,' he says.

He keeps shrugging the jacket back, then tugging it forward again.

'I just need somebody,' he says. 'Is that wrong?'

My turn to sigh. Like I said, we're still drafting the rulebook. The last one we had got buried with Mum.

'John, you wouldn't give me a hand with this would you?' Dad bleats plaintively.

I do his tie for him.

'Once upon a time,' he says, 'I used to do this for you.'

Forget it, Dad. You're not going to go all sentimental on me.

'No, you didn't,' I say, squashing his lame attempt at male bonding.

'I did too!'

'No, Dad,' I tell him firmly. 'You didn't. I wore sweat shirts at primary school and it was Mum who showed me how to do my tie when I got to High School. Scrub Tony Parsons and Nick Hornby, it was definitely a Mum and Boy thing.'

'So I never did?'

There's hurt in his voice but I'm in no mood to give him an easy way out.

'No.'

Come to think of it, he didn't do much of anything else, either. It was Mum who took us swimming, Mum who took us to Pizza Hut, Mum who helped us with our homework. The only big landmark that involved Dad was when I learned to ride my bike. He was the one who was holding the seat when I came off and left half my face on the tarmac round the rec. Not that it was his fault, missing most of our big days. He always seemed to be working. Overtime was his middle name.

'Funny,' he says. 'I remember it vividly.'

'Odd how the mind plays tricks, isn't it?' I observe, with just a dash of pepper in my voice.

He glances at the kitchen clock. It's a quarter to eight.

'What time are you meeting her?' I ask.

Dad brightens as if I've just given my blessing. Think again. I'm just making conversation.

'I'm picking her up from her place at half past eight.'

'Where does she live?'

'Over the water. Heswall.'

'Better get a move on, hadn't you?'

'How can I?' he says. 'Our Gary isn't back yet. Where is the little toe-rag? I told him seven o'clock!'

'I'll chase him up for you,' I say. 'Just get going.'

Dad hesitates.

'I'd better not,' he says, finally. 'I need him home before I set foot out of this door.'

You can understand why: Gary's been on the slide for weeks. He never lets on what he's up to, but you can guarantee it's bad news. Ever since Mum died, Dad's been taking this parenting lark really seriously, but Gary's getting further and further away from him. Why can't he see it? Or is it that he doesn't want to see it?

'Honestly, Dad,' I tell him. 'I'll track Gary down. You go.'

I can't quite bring myself to add: *and have a good time*.

'Are you sure, John lad?'

'Sure I'm sure.'

'I'll phone you,' he says. 'I've got my mobile.'

'Don't worry,' I say. 'Gary's bound to be home soon.'

'Yes,' says Dad. 'Of course he will.'

I watch from the door as he walks to the car. He's still worried about our Gary so I smile reassuringly, like a parent sending their kid off to school on their first day. It's only when Dad has turned left into the main road that I allow the cosmetic smile to fade.

Gary, where are you?

I do my homework until nine o'clock. It's GCSE coursework on the PC so I sit in the kitchen-cum-dining room typing away with the light off. I like it this way, watching the twilight fade, the trees gradually losing their shape and becoming patches of deep-dark against the half-dark of the city night. This way I can imagine I'm living deep in a mysterious forest, the house filled with the scent of pine, or in a beach house on a South Sea island, wind chimes jangling in the balmy ocean breeze. So long as I type, cushioned by the darkness, I'm not in the middle of Liverpool in a three-bedroom semi that backs onto the Northern Line. I suppose I must come across as a bit of a saddo doing my homework on Friday night. The weekend has hardly begun but I've already done most of it. But that's me, the John-that-Mum-built. Don't let it pile up, she would say, break the back of it on Friday night and you've got the rest of the weekend to yourself. She had a word for it: diligent. So that's the way I'll always be: diligent.

For her.

You know how diligent I am? I'm so diligent that I'm not even going to try to chat Olivia Bellman up until tomorrow and she's gorgeous. I'm getting my homework out of the way first. Yes, when it comes to school I'm a natural. When I was eleven, Mum put me down for St Thomas's. It's the school everybody tries to get their kids into. Competition is so fierce they have an entrance exam. We're talking camels and the eye of a needle. The day I did the test and interview most of the kids turned up in BMWs, Range Rovers or top of the range Volvos. Mum drove me down in our red Fiesta. Well, most of it was red. The door was green on account of a bump we had, GBH by White Van Man. Dad got the green door from a scrapyard to save money. It was nine months before he got round to re-spraying it. Mum said the car had gone through a full-term pregnancy. We got a few funny looks as we pulled into the car park but I passed the test and sailed through the interview. Mum was proud as punch. My son the brainbox.

It wasn't like that with our Gary.

Like I said, we're like chalk and cheese. He never took to school. He was the duck that was allergic to water. In playgroup he coloured all his pictures black. I think his teacher was about to tattoo his skull with the old 666 when he moved up to reception. In the infants, he reluctantly added a bit of red to his "studies in black" but he didn't really do much else. When you get banned from the sand tray after just two weeks, you know you're not in line for a glittering career.

By the time he entered the juniors he was going downhill fast. One time, Mum brought his workbooks home from parents' evening. On half the pages, he'd written the date but not much else. She wasn't too keen to bring his work home after that, but she plugged away, trying get through to him. It was always Mum, never Dad, not that Dad seems to realise that.

Once Gary got to High School – not mine, of course, the one up the road, the one with the cracked windows, peeling paintwork and hot and cold running scallies – only Mum's best efforts kept him in the place at all. She said he was school-phobic and needed support. Dad said he was a little plonker and needed a toe up his backside. The support finally carried the day over the toe. Thanks to Mum, Gary ended up with a certificate for 100 per cent attendance and his name in the *Echo*.

'At least the lad turns up,' his form teacher said. 'All we've got to do now is get some work out of him while he's here.'

Talking of turning up, where is he? When Dad phoned I covered for him. *Yes, he's here*, I answered brightly through my lying teeth. He wasn't, and he isn't now. What's more, he's got his mobile switched off and I've tried every one of his mates without success.

What are you up to, Gary? What on earth are you up to?

It's ten o'clock. I'm starting to get anxious. I mean, I told Dad Gary was already in. What if the old man comes home early and he isn't here? Then it won't just be Gary who gets it in the neck. If the little rat gets me grounded and I miss out on Olivia Bellman I swear I'll kill him. I peer through the curtains. This must be what it's like to be a parent. The moment our Gary gets in from school he's off out with his mates and he never gets in on time. At first he would be five or ten minutes late. Now he goes missing for hours on end. Dad breathes a lot of fire but Gary knows he can get away with it and usually does.

I go upstairs to put my coursework folder in my room. I'm about to go back down when I happen to glance out the window and catch sight of Gary. There he is, walking up the street away from the house. That does it! I'm not missing out on Olivia Bellman on your account, Gary Cain. I fly downstairs, grab my key and shoot out the door.

'Gary!'

He's almost at the top of the street before I catch up with him. He's strolling along with two other lads. They're wearing regulation baseball caps and doing the same walk, a kind of rappers' shuffle they've picked up off MTV.

'Gary, wait up.'

He finally stops and turns round. He looks at me like I just crawled out of the grid.

'What's with you?' he asks.

'I'll tell you what's with me,' I say, sounding more like

the old man all the time. 'You promised to be back for seven.'

'Dad's out,' says Gary. 'What he doesn't know won't hurt him. I'll be in before eleven so stop worrying.'

'What if Dad gets back first?'

'He won't. He's out with his new tart, isn't he?'

Tart! Mum would have killed him for talking like that. The two other lads snigger. I run an eye over them. One I recognise, a pasty weasel of a kid by the name of Sean Pike. The other one's older, late teens, and I've never seen him before.

'I wouldn't let Dad hear you saying that,' I say. 'She's probably very nice.'

'Yes,' Gary says scornfully. '*Nice.*'

'Make sure you're back before eleven,' I tell him.

'OK,' he says, '*Mum.*'

I catch his eye. Still playing to the gallery, are you Gaz?

'You know what, Gary,' I snap back. 'You're sick.'

He flinches, but when his mates give their appreciative chuckle his backbone stiffens.

He walks away leaving me seething with impotent fury.

It's ten past eleven.

Ten past.

Gary, you're taking the—

The door goes.

'G—'

I manage to choke the word off before I give myself away. But it isn't Gary. It's Dad. He turns the key in the lock behind him and heads for the kitchen. He doesn't say a word. I steal up to the door. With all the care and delicacy of a bomb disposal expert, I turn the key back so as not to alert Dad to the missing brother. I've got to leave it open for Gary.

Come on you divvy, get a move on.

'So how was it?' I ask, keen to field any awkward questions about my moron of a kid brother.

Dad shrugs.

'The food was nice.'

'What did you have?'

'Indian.'

I can almost taste Chicken Dhansak.

'I like Indian.'

I try to read his expression. I don't have much luck. The *Man in the Iron Mask*, that's Dad.

'And her?'

'She's a nice girl.'

Nice, just like Gary said.

Dad struggles out of his tie, the one I did for him, and hangs it over the back of the chair. He looks defeated.

'I'm going to bed,' he says wearily even though it's only quarter past eleven. 'You lock the back door and put the alarm on.'

Halfway upstairs I hear his voice.

'Goodnight, Gary,' he calls.

A band of horror snaps round my heart. Now I'm for it.

'Goodnight, Dad,' Gary answers.

I do a double-take. Gary's in! Where did he come from?

'It's good to see you in at a reasonable hour,' says Dad. 'Well done, lad.'

Just listen to him! Gary somehow sneaks in at the last minute and puts on an act and he's the one who collects all the Brownie points. As for me, Mr Rotten Sensible, I cover for the rat and worry myself sick half the night. What do I get for my trouble? *You lock up*.

I do it, of course. I lock up, switch off the lights and set the alarm. Like I said, I'm diligent. I'm crossing the landing to my room when Gary pops his head round the door.

'Thanks for leaving the door open,' he whispers. 'I just

21

had time to nip upstairs and dive into bed. I owe you one, John.'

One? You owe me a lot more than that, our kid.

Next morning, I'm up at eight o'clock even though it's Saturday. I shower and examine the latest crater cluster of spots. My face looks more like the Sea of Tranquility every day. Ever since I was fourteen I've been suffering nuclear bombardment by hormones.

Somehow, in spite of testosterone overload, I've got to look my best today. Olivia Bellman never looks anything but her best. Immaculate is what she is. Her parents are doctors and she wears nothing but the latest fashions. She will be holding court in Church Street around eleven and I plan to get there early. Third suitor from the left, that's me. Olivia doesn't know I know she'll be in Church Street. In fact, I'm not even sure she knows I exist, but I plan to bump into her accidentally-on-purpose.

You should see this girl. She's got long, blonde hair way down her back and these huge, vivid blue eyes that can freeze-frame a heartbeat at twenty paces. She is, as my best mate Adam Jones would say, *the business*. I've been an admirer of Olivia for at least a million years, well, since the start of Year 8 anyway. But I've hardly said a word to her. I've never *dared*. On the scale of evolution I'm amoeba and she's Helen of Troy. All that ends today though. On this, the third of May, I will declare my intentions to make the lovely Olivia mine.

I make my way along the landing past Gary's pit. He's sleeping with the curtains open as usual. He's too lazy even to draw them. His door is ajar and I can see a litter of crisp packets, drinks cans, yoghurt cartons and odd socks on the floor. Dad laid a laminated wooden floor for Gary three years ago on account of him getting a touch of asthma. Mum reckoned the dust would have fewer places to gather

22

if we replaced the carpet with a wooden floor. You wouldn't be able to tell *what* sort of floor he had now, though. The snack litter is now so thick the pine doesn't even show through the gunk zone.

'You awake Gary?' I ask.

'Nn-guh,' comes the Cro-Magnon reply.

On a Saturday, life as the rest of us know it doesn't visit Gary's room until noon, at least.

'Gaz.'

Why should he get a lie-in anyway? He had me on tenterhooks all yesterday evening and now he thinks he can just lie rotting in his pit as if nothing's happened.

'Gary!'

'Nn-guh-huh?'

But Dad's voice cuts short the futile attempt to raise the undead from his crypt.

'Knock it off, John. Let the lad sleep.'

Will you listen to that? *I* get my homework finished, *I* take care of the house, *I* cover for His Lordship and who does Dad side with? What is this, good guys come last? Sure, I said I'd be there for Gary, but I didn't sign up for martyrdom. I give Gary's door a last accusing stare and return to the bathroom. It's the spots. I can't go chatting up Olivia Bellman with a face like a blister-pack. But what do I do about it?

After locking the door I start searching through the bathroom cabinet. TCP, that ought to do something. Bracing myself, I dab it undiluted onto the offending spots. I don't know which is worse, the sting or the stench. But I'm set on shock therapy. *Out, damned spots!* You have to tell zits who's the boss. I rub Vic on them next, then follow that up with a couple of alcohol wipes. That should do something.

Out, I say again, *out damned spots!*

I rinse my face and look in the mirror. Other than

23

making my eyes water, the anti-zit campaign doesn't seem to have had much effect. No, I tell a lie, it's making my face glow like a hundred-watt bulb. Oh no, now I'm a refugee from a nuclear power plant. I'm about to give up and go down for breakfast when I hear Gary snoring like a happy pig.

That does it.

Why should he sleep the day away after last night? By way of revenge for his thoughtlessness and laziness I pick up his toothbrush and start scrubbing away at my spots. Lousy hormones, stinking zits, stupid brother! With a wicked grin I put the brush back in the holder, unwashed. It might not cure my spots but the idea of Gary putting *that* in his mouth sure makes me feel better!

Dad's in the kitchen.

'You're up early,' I say.

'This isn't early,' Dad says. 'I'm up at six on a weekday.'

'Early for a weekend then.'

I watch him making breakfast, trying to work out from his body language how the date went. Right now, I hope it was an unqualified disaster. Who does he think he is, swanning off with some typist while I'm stuck trying to sort Gary out? Isn't there any justice in this world? Unable to read the signs, Dad being a pretty neutral sort of breakfast-maker, I decide to come right out with it.

'Well,' I say. 'Are you seeing her again?'

Dad shakes his head.

'How come? Don't you like her?'

'She's fine.'

'What then?'

Suddenly I'm in a playful mood.

'Is she boring? Has she got a wooden leg? A third eye? Bigamist? Polygamist? I know, she's an alien from the planet Zergon.'

'John, she's lovely, a really lovely girl.'

I can't say I want to hear this. I stop goofing around. Still, I'm curious about what happened.

'So—?'

'I blew it.'

'How?'

'I talked about your mother.'

Suddenly I feel quite good about my dad.

'I didn't plan it,' he says. 'But she asked me about Lisa. She's the one who got me started, you see. The trouble is, I couldn't stop. I droned on and on about Lisa, how beautiful she was, what a good mother she was, how much I missed her, the hatred I've got for that drunk driver. I even talked about her favourite music. It was only when she started looking at her watch that I realised quite how long I must have been going on.'

You know what, Dad, you're not so bad after all.

'So you're not seeing her again?' I ask, just a bit too eagerly.

Dad shakes his head ruefully. I can't say I'm shedding any tears.

'Short of applying thumbscrews, I don't think I could have given her a more uncomfortable evening.'

He sighs and takes a gulp of sweet, milky tea from his Homer Simpson mug.

'Maybe you were right last night,' I say. 'It's too early to be seeing someone new.'

Dad seems to agree, but he doesn't look too happy about it.

'Gary's still in bed then?' he says, changing the subject.

'Yes.'

'I'm just relieved he was in early. I've been getting really worried about him lately. I'm not keen on the company he's been keeping. Touch wood he's turned the corner.'

Suddenly, there's this Jiminy Cricket voice inside my

head yelling : *Tell him!* But I decide against it. I'm diligent but not that diligent. Nobody likes a snitch.

'Yes,' I say. 'You never know.'

2

Adam and I meet at Orrell Park station. It's a funny place, Orrell Park, a huddle of ageing townhouses in the north end of the city. It was quite well off at one time. Some of the houses still have buzzers in the living room, a reminder of the days when the residents had servants but those days are long gone. There are no bankers and merchants here these days. Most people are in work, but only your common or garden manual and clerical jobs. Working, but not really comfortable. Most of the local kids call the area 'Orrible Park, but it isn't too bad.

'Are you sure about this?' he asks.

'Of course.'

'Really and truly 100 per cent sure?'

'Adam, I'm positive.'

He shakes his head.

'Well, don't blame me when it all goes pear-shaped. I'm starting to wish I'd never overheard that she was going to town today.'

'Adam,' I say. 'What makes you think something's going to go wrong?'

Olivia Bellman is one of the few bright spots in my life just now. Today *can't* go wrong.

'John, we're talking about Olivia Bellman here. *Olivia Bellman.*'

'Yes, I know.'

'Setting your sights a bit high, aren't you? I mean, she's seriously gorgeous. She can take her pick of the lads and

27

she's never looked twice at anybody below the sixth form.'

I dig him in the ribs.

'Are you trying to tell me I'm not worthy?'

'What I'm saying, John, is none of us are. The girl's family is minted, she looks like something out of the *FHM* "100 List" and she's been known to eat bigger lads than you for breakfast.'

Olivia, I think, I'll be your bacon rasher anytime. I hear the train rumbling into the platform.

'Come on, we're going to miss it.'

We run over the footbridge and file in behind the other passengers. It's standing room only. At the next station a few people get off and we find a seat. I start telling Adam about Gary.

'Sean Pike, you say?'

'That's right. Why, do you know him?'

'Sean, no. But if he's related to the Norris Green Pikes he's bad news. Find out if he's got an older brother called Eddie. My mum taught him a few years ago. She was always going on about him. He gave her a dog's life.'

Adam's mum teaches at our Gary's school. The board outside says: '*Achievement for all*.' Hah! '*Lose hope all ye who enter herein*' might be more like it. I once asked Adam if he knew how Gary was doing. Adam told me he'd rather not say in case he incriminated himself. I think it's called 'Taking the Fifth Amendment'.

'So what's the score with Eddie Pike now?'

'He's in Walton prison. He did some fellow over in a pub. Hospitalized him, by all accounts.'

'Does he look like a weasel?'

'What?'

'This Eddie Pike, does he look like a weasel? Only Sean does. He's got eyes like pinheads and the longest, pointiest nose you've ever seen in your life.'

'I've no idea what he looks like,' Adam says. 'But I can ask Mum for you.'

Listening to Adam talking about the Pikes, and thinking about the effect Sean might be having on my stupid, lost brother, I get an uneasy feeling. Like night is coming.

We're coming out of the station when we bump into Yvette Tomlinson. She's in my form, the only other kid from my primary school who got into St Thomas's. We used to play together when we were little but the Tomlinsons moved out of the area to one of the new riverside estates nearer town, so I don't see her so often outside school.

Still, I suppose she's the nearest thing I'll ever get to a sister. She seems really glad to see me. Funny thing, I've always thought of Yvette not only as a sister, but as a kid-sister, her being head and shoulders shorter than me, but out of uniform she's quite something.

She's on the way to being a woman all right. There's her shape, which is usually disguised by the St Thomas uniform, and the mane of long, curly auburn hair. But there's plenty that still makes her my sort-of-kid-sister. You can hardly get a pin between the freckles on her nose and cheeks. Yvette's also got cheeks like a hamster. She probably hates her freckles the same way I hate my zits. And those chubby cheeks, they make her look fifteen-going-on-five. Being on the short side definitely doesn't help. So that's Yvette, one quarter woman, three quarters kid-sister and four quarters one of the nicest people I've known in my whole life.

'Hi John, Adam.'

'Yvette.'

The moment she smiles I notice something new. It's her teeth. She's got some of those colourless braces, which explains her absence from school yesterday afternoon. Yvette starts curling her lip over her teeth the way a tapir does at the zoo. She's obviously really self-conscious about the braces. I want to ask her where she got it done. I had to see the orthodontist a few weeks ago and he's threatening me with some. Braces and multi-zits. That would spell the end of life as I know it.

'Meeting somebody?' she asks.

'He's got the hots for Olivia Bellman,' says Adam, digging me in the ribs.

Maybe I'm imagining it but for a moment Yvette looks crushed. Without quite knowing why, I glare at Adam.

'Well,' he says. 'You have.'

Brain to fingers: strangle Adam the first chance you get.

'O-liv-i-aaa!' he adds in a mock-posh accent.

'We're just having a wander round,' I say, wondering if my orthodontist could arrange a jaw brace for Adam. 'You?'

'I'm with my mum.'

Mum is the plump, five-foot nothing, hamster-cheeked redhead standing a few yards away, smiling at me.

'Hello, Yvette's mum,' I say.

'Hello, John,' she replies, then, glancing at Yvette, 'We'd better make a move, love.'

Yvette gives me a self-conscious smile and jogs after her mum.

'You could do worse,' says Adam.

'Come again?'

'Yvette Tomlinson. She's nice and she likes you.'

Me and Yvette? No, we're friends. You don't go out with a best friend. It's not right. Besides, I could imagine how it would go down at school. The Alpha males give you grief if your girlfriend doesn't come up to scratch. Just think what they'd make of Yvette. I can already hear the *Jaws* jokes.

'Behave,' I tell him. 'My heart belongs to Olivia Bellman.'

30

We start crossing the road towards Church Street. I can't help feeling annoyed with myself somehow.

'It's your funeral,' says Adam. 'Don't say I didn't warn you.'

I spot Olivia immediately. She's sitting with Gillian Hill, Kedra Powell and Philippa Blake. Yipes! That's the entire Paradise Set in one go. Paradise Set is the name we give to St Thomas's most eligible females because that's what they're like: four gorgeous Birds of Paradise.

'Told you she'd be here,' says Adam. 'Go get her, tiger.'

He's taking the mickey so I ignore him.

'Well, what's holding you back?'

'Just in case you hadn't noticed,' I answer frostily. 'There are four of them.'

I saw a documentary about this once, how lions isolate a single wildebeest from the herd. Not that I'm comparing Olivia Bellman to a wildebeest, you understand. Heaven forbid! Anyway, about these lions. The pride charges the herd and the male singles out the juiciest prey. But Olivia is a lot more unapproachable than any wildebeest and, instead of a pride, all I've got is Adam.

'Can't you chat up the other three for me?' I ask. 'You know, distract them.'

'Who do you think I am?' Adam asks. 'Superstud? How exactly do I chat them all up at once?'

'I don't know. Charm?'

Adam laughs.

'John, charm I've got. But godlike powers, no chance.'

'So what do I do?'

'Do like the rest of us,' Adam says. 'Yearn from afar, John. Yearn from afar.'

But I've done yearning, lots of it. I've yearned through English, desired through History, longed through French,

31

sighed through Maths. Stuff yearning, what I want is snogging!

'Tell you what,' I say. 'We'll just kind of saunter past, pretend we haven't noticed them.'

'So now we're after an Oscar nomination,' says Adam. 'How exactly do we pretend we haven't noticed the Paradise Set? What do you think I am, dead?'

Eventually, he agrees to give it a go. We walk down Church Street towards the statue where they are gathered. We're just approaching when Kedra spots Adam.

'Hello there, Adam,' she says.

'Hello, Kedra.'

Nobody adds '*Hello, John.*' Suddenly, I'm the Invisible Man. I just give this gawky smile and we carry on walking.

'Well, that went well,' says Adam shaking his head. 'I was really impressed by your chat-up line. What's with you? Couldn't you think of *anything* to say?'

I give a mournful shake of the head.

'Do you mean we came all the way into town for *that*!'

I glance back just as Gillian makes some comment about us and the four of them burst out laughing. I turn so red, my spots fade into the background.

We spend the next ten minutes outside HMV, arguing tactics. Adam has been encouraged by Kedra's 'hello' and wants to go and see if there's anything to it. So, back down Church Street we go. By the time we get to the statue, all my confidence has drained out of me. Everything was OK so long as Olivia was only a fantasy. But the moment I tried to substitute the girl for the idea everything went belly up. We arrive at the statue to discover it has been taken over by a load of Goths: all white foundation, black lipstick and long, shapeless clothes, black, of course. Adam shapes his fingers into a cross. The latter-day vampires snarl back.

'Dead original, aren't you?'

I have no interest in Goth-baiting.

'So where'd Olivia go?' I ask, looking round.

Adam shrugs. That's when we hear a voice behind us.

'Looking for somebody?'

It's Olivia.

She has this superior smile playing on her lips. Gillian, Kedra and Philippa are whispering behind their hands. Adam helpfully leaves the talking to me.

'Yes, er—'

'Who?'

Olivia is smiling. The Paradise Set are giggling.

'Well not some*body* actually . . .'

Stutter. Stammer. How did I get myself into this?

'Some*where*.'

I look around for inspiration.

'We were looking for—'

Ping! The electric light goes on in my head.

'Littlewoods!'

Brilliant!

'Yes, we're looking for Littlewoods.'

Adam groans. Obviously not brilliant.

'Littlewoods?' says Olivia, half-turning to indicate the huge store behind us. 'You mean *that*?'

I stare at it, the mighty building that dominates the centre of Church Street, much as the White House dominates Pennsylvania Avenue. Definitely not brilliant. In fact, just about the lamest thing I've ever said.

'Oh yes—'

Face glowing scarlet. Stomach flipping. Legs turning to jelly.

'—there it is.'

Adam is willing himself to sink into the ground.

'See you,' I say, hurrying away.

And we're talking about *Bat out of Hell* retreat. By the time anyone speaks I'm almost running.

'Yes,' says Olivia. 'See you.'

The Paradise Set dissolve into helpless laughter behind us.

'So we were looking for Littlewoods, were we?' Adam asks.

I look out of the compartment window as our train rumbles past the docks. My breath clouds the window. Through the condensation I see the Mersey ferry chugging across the river and think of Dad proposing to Mum.

'OK,' I say. 'You can knock it off now. You've made your point.'

'Littlewoods!' says Adam, pretending to jump as if he'd found the building lurking behind him. 'Where did that come from?'

At last I'm starting to see the funny side.

'I suppose it was pretty obvious.'

'You can say that again.'

I punch him on the arm. He socks me back. We're pounding each other to dull the pain of defeat. The ferry disappears from view.

By the time we get home, Gary is just getting up.

'Do you know the time?' I ask accusingly, still stressed-out by the Bellman fiasco.

'No, *Mum*. Why don't you tell me.'

'You can cut that out too,' I snarl.

'What?'

'Calling me Mum. In the circumstances, I'd say that's in pretty bad taste, wouldn't you?'

No answer, but I think he's got the point.

'Where is Dad anyway?' I ask.

Gary shrugs and turns his back. I glance at Adam. He just shakes his head.

'What's eating little brother?'

34

It's my turn to shrug.

'Didn't Dad say anything before he went out?'

By now, Gary is swigging from a two-litre carton of milk. He wouldn't have got away with *that* when Mum was here. With her it was always, *use a cup, Gary*. But she isn't here, and she never will be again. Sometimes it's hard to get my head round that.

'How should I know? I was asleep.'

'You never do anything else lately,' I say.

Gary leaves the empty carton on the side.

'Aren't you going to put that in the bin?' I ask.

Gary rolls his eyes.

'No, I'm going out.'

Frustrated, I bin the carton. The front door slams.

'He's really starting to get on my nerves.'

Adam nods.

'I can see why.'

Dad arrives home.

'Has Adam gone?' he asks.

'Yes.'

'Gary?'

'He's out.'

'Any idea where?'

What am I, his personal secretary?

'No, just out.'

'Didn't you even ask him?' Dad grumbles.

'Oh, I asked,' I say. 'It doesn't mean he answered.'

'Have you two been arguing again?'

I don't even grace that with a reply. Why does he always have to paint me as the bad guy?

'I'm going to put my foot down,' says Dad.

Yes, sure you are.

'Has he done his homework?'

This is getting tedious!

'How should *I* know?' I say. 'But he was only just crawling out of bed when I got in.'

Dad marches to the phone.

'That does it,' he says. 'I'm getting him home to do it. I've started getting nasty letters from the school. You'd think it was my fault.'

Yes, you would, wouldn't you!

I hear him punching out Gary's mobile number. Dad slams down the receiver.

'He's got it switched off again!' Dad snaps. 'What's the point of him having the damned thing?'

Dad isn't talking to me. He's just venting his anger.

'Any chance of you tracking him down?' he asks.

Wonderful, first I'm a personal secretary, now I'm a rotten detective agency!

'I'll try.'

I've been riding round on my bike trying to track Gary down when I come across Mick Fraser. Mick's been Gary's best mate since dinosaurs walked the Earth.

'Mick!' I shout. 'Hey Mick, over here.'

For some reason, the look he gives me sets my nerves jangling.

'Hello there, John. You all right?'

'Fine. I'm looking for our Gary.'

'Can't help you there, John. I haven't seen him.'

'Oh,' I say, disappointed. 'I was sure he'd be at yours.'

Mick wrinkles his nose.

'Living in the past, aren't you, John?'

He waits a beat then explains.

'Look, you may not know, but we don't hang around much any more. Gary doesn't want to know me since he started knocking round with his new mates.'

For some reason it feels like I've got cobwebs all over me. My skin's prickling.

36

'What new mates are these?' I ask, dreading the answer.

'Sean Pike, Tony Connolly.'

He reels off their names before taking a deep breath.

'Then there's Adrian Healey.'

'Who's he?'

Mick stops making eye contact.

'I don't know much about him. He drives a car, though, so he's got to be seventeen at least.'

There's an alarm going off in my head. Seventeen. I don't like the sound of that so it's a sure bet Dad won't be happy either.

'What's somebody his age doing hanging round with a fourteen-year-old?'

Mick shakes his head.

'Beats me, especially after what happened on the bridge.'

'After *what* happened on the bridge?'

Mick realises he has said too much.

'I'd better not—'

I block his way.

'Come on, cough.'

'OK,' says Mick, reluctantly. 'It was the week before last. We were up on the bridge, the one over Rice Lane.'

I'm getting a sinking feeling.

'Adrian was with us. He started dropping bombs on the cars.'

'Bombs?'

Mick nods.

'You know – balloons filled with water.'

'Doesn't sound so heavy.'

'Yes, but then he lets a bottle go.'

'What, a glass one?'

'Budweiser bottle. We'd all been drinking. Well, it smashed all over the front of a Merc. We did a runner but I got caught. The coppers brought me home. Dad went ballistic.'

'I bet you kept your mouth shut about the others, though.'

'What do you expect?' Mick asks. 'I'm no grass. Anyway, I've been grounded for the last fortnight. This is my first day out.'

'So, Gary and this Adrian got away with it?'

Mick nods.

'I thought it would have got back to your dad somehow though. My old man said he was going to have a word.'

'Well, he hasn't,' I tell Mick. 'There'd be blood on the walls if he knew.'

Thank goodness for overtime, that's what I say. Just lately Dad's out before seven and back late.

'Don't let on I told you,' says Mick. 'Adrian doesn't like people who grass. He's a bit of a hard knock. You wouldn't want to cross him.'

I don't answer. I get back on my bike and ride away wondering what to say to Dad.

Gary finally turns up at half past ten.

'Where have you been?' Dad demands, meeting him at the front door.

'Out.'

There's an intake of breath.

'I know that. Where, though, and who were you with?'

'You know, around, with my mates.'

Dad glances at me as if expecting moral support. I look away. I haven't told him about my chat with Mick and I'm feeling as guilty as hell. Plus I think it's Dad's job, not mine. I mean, who's the adult round here? The third degree goes on for about five minutes, pretty unsuccessfully, I have to say. Dad mentions Mick's name at one point and Gary flinches visibly. Not that Dad notices. He's too busy with his interrogation.

'So what do Michael's parents say about this, hanging round till all hours?'

Gary recovers quickly.

'They're cool. Half past ten isn't late, anyway.'

I stare at him. Since when did he become such an accomplished liar?

'It's not like when you were young, you know.'

Dad grinds his teeth.

'That's half the trouble,' he says. 'Anyway, what did you do for tea?'

'I had a Mackie's.'

That's a McDonald's to the kids round here.

'Do you want anything now?'

'I'll get a bowl of cereal after,' says Gary, heading for the PC.

'Oh, no you don't,' says Dad. 'If you want any supper get it now. And you're not playing games on that computer. It's bedtime. Oh yes, one more thing, you don't leave this house tomorrow until you've done your homework.'

Gary pulls a face. That sets Dad off again.

'Understood?'

This time Gary stares at the floor. His inner spring is being coiled tight.

'I asked if you understood.'

The inner spring snaps back. Gary's voice rasps with anger.

'I understand, OK! Now can I get past?'

Dad steps to one side and watches Gary climb the stairs. He knows that Gary is like a ship lying at anchor when a storm is coming. One by one, the mooring ropes snap and the vessel begins to drift. Dad isn't stupid. He can hear the mooring ropes breaking as well as I can. He turns my way with a face like thunder.

'You've got fifteen minutes, John.'

39

The way he says it, you'd think I was the one who was tearing the family to bits, instead of the poor mug who's trying to hold it together.

3

I wake up thinking about Olivia Bellman. I lie in bed smiling at the thought of her. She's like a ghost hovering above me in my room, and what a ghost! The way the curtains move in the early morning breeze reminds me of her hair. Then I remember yesterday and the smile vanishes from my face. She must think I'm a complete moron. Oh God, I live all my life in Liverpool and I ask her where Littlewoods is! I climb out of bed wincing at the thought of the humiliation to come. I need to pee so I go to the bathroom. The door is locked.

'Dad?'

'No, it's me.'

Gary unlocks the door and tries to walk past. Less than happy with the hand life has dealt me, I launch into him. I shove him against the door jamb and jab a finger in his face. He isn't impressed. He goes deadpan. Determined to get my point across, I hiss a warning.

'Are you going to tell me what you're up to?'

'What are you on about?'

'I know about the water bombs.'

He stares, then smiles. Somehow, put like that, it doesn't sound serious at all.

'And the bottle.'

He pouts an excuse.

'I didn't drop it.'

'No, it was Adrian.'

Now Gary knows the source of my information.

'Mick told you, didn't he?'

'That's right. You do realise that Dad'll kill you when he finds out.'

'But he isn't going to find out, is he?'

Gary's becoming really hard-faced. This is the kid who once cried over a dead bird in the back garden. The kid who, once upon a time when Mum was alive and we were still some kind of family, wouldn't walk to the video shop on his own in case there was a gang hanging round.

What's happened to you, Gary?

'You're not going to grass though, are you?' he says.

He waits for a moment then brushes past with a smirk.

'I thought not.'

By the time Dad comes down for breakfast I've already washed up. I'm reading *A Kestrel for a Knave*. Nothing like a slice of urban misery to remind me there are people worse off than I am.

'Schoolwork?' he asks.

'No, pleasure. Adam's mum lent it to me.'

I show Dad her name inside the front cover. She's dated it too. I like that. I think I'll start dating my books. Who knows, years from now, when I'm a poet or a screenwriter, I might look back and see how it all began.

'I saw the film,' Dad says. '*Kes*. It was good, especially the football match.'

I smile back. I can just see Billy Casper shivering in goal.

'Adam's mum says the best bit is where Billy describes putting his foot in a Wellington boot full of tadpoles.'

'Kind of reminds you of life,' says Dad. 'That's a bit like sticking your foot in a boot full of tadpoles.'

I think of Olivia. I'd swim through an *ocean* of tadpoles for her.

'Do you want any bacon?' Dad asks.

'No, I've just had Shreddies.'

42

'Is my laddo still in bed?'

'I think so.'

Dad laughs.

'You know what my old man did if I stayed in bed too long?'

I shake my head. (I do but – what the heck – why not humour him?)

'He'd take a flannel soaked in cold water, pull back the bedclothes, and slap it against the small of my back. Worked every time.'

I look at him. OK, so your dad was some kind of sadist.

'Your point being?'

'My point,' says Dad, 'is that I had firm rules to go by when I was a lad.'

He turns the bacon in the pan.

'I'm not sure our Gary does.'

I want to give him a good shake. *So whose fault is that, Dad?* No need to beat him up over it, though. He starts doing that himself.

'Your mum always knew what to do,' he says. 'I wish I did.'

Oh, for crying out loud! Spare me the self-pity.

'How can two brothers be so different?' Dad wonders out loud. 'Hanging round the streets isn't your style, is it?'

'I do go out,' I protest.

I mean, give me a break, I don't want to come across as a dork.

'Yes,' says Dad. 'But you've always got something to do.'

Yes, like stalking Olivia Bellman.

'Let's face it, John, you're more of a home boy than Gary. You've got your schoolwork, your computer games, reading . . .'

Now he's struggling. I've never been the sporty type. Mum and Dad tried me with football but that wasn't my

43

thing. Then it was judo but that wasn't my thing either. After ill-fated attempts at tennis and competitive swimming they seem to have accepted that sport isn't really my thing. Gary, on the other hand, is a natural. He was in the school football team until Year 9 and he briefly represented Walton in swimming. Then the hormones kicked in. Dad had a half-hearted go at persuading him to carry on with the sport, but Gary always found a way out. For the last eleven months he hasn't done any of it. As soon as Mum was gone, he dropped the lot.

'Has Gary said anything to you?' Dad asks.

Oh, here we go.

'What about?'

'Where he goes at night. What he's getting up to.'

'No, not really. He's just hanging round with his mates.'

What's the point of saying what I know? It's not as though Dad would know how to sort it out.

I spend the day at Adam's. We watch *Billy Elliott* on video.

'This some kind of holy mission you've got going?' I ask Mrs Jones.

'How do you mean?'

'Bit of a running theme, isn't there? The kid who needs a guiding hand to fulfill his dreams.'

I'm thinking about *Kes* and our Gary, though I can't see him taking up falconry or ballet. Gary in a tutu? Not much street cred there.

'You could be right,' Mrs Jones says. 'That's what got me into teaching, the idea that I could make a difference.'

'And do you?'

She sighs and I hear the echoes of a hundred switched-off scallies in her voice.

'Not as much as I'd like. A lot of our kids don't even want to be in school, never mind learn anything.'

Adam's dad pats her on the arm.

'Don't put yourself down. You're a good teacher.'

'It doesn't matter how good you are,' she says. 'You can't get through to everyone.'

Here's my chance. I'm in like a shot.

'Do you get through to the Pikes?' I ask.

'What makes you ask?'

'Gary's knocking round with Sean Pike.'

Her expression changes.

'You don't think it's such a good idea, do you?'

'John, I can't . . .'

'Be honest, you don't.'

'No,' she says. 'I don't. Sean Pike is a troubled young man.' (Translation: vicious little psychopath.) 'I think Gary ought to pick his friends more carefully.'

'So you're worried about him?'

'I wouldn't go that far.'

'No,' I say, my expression gauge changing from neutral to glum. 'But I would.'

When I get home, the house seems empty, but it can't be. The alarm is off.

'Dad?'

It isn't worth calling Gary. He's bound to be out.

'Dad, are you in?'

The back door is ajar. So that's it. He's in the wash-house. Our house is a hundred years old so we've got a wash-house round the back. It's why Mum picked it, so she could stick the washing machine and tumble drier out there. I step outside and knock on the door. I've done that ever since I walked in on Mum once and nearly gave her a heart attack. Before I know it, I'm leaning my head on the door. I can still feel her presence in every molecule of this house. I pull myself together and call through the door.

'Dad?'

'Oh, hi there, John lad.'

He seems to have calmed down since last night.

'Do you need a hand?' I ask, safe in the knowledge that he doesn't.

'No, I'm finished here.'

He props open the door and emerges with a plastic laundry basket.

'Last lap,' he says. 'Just the ironing to do.'

He sighs.

'I hate ironing.'

I can still remember the first lot he did. That's one Liverpool replica shirt that will never recover. Twenty minutes he was scrubbing the iron with a brillo to get the melted polyester off. Still, it could have been worse – it was Gary's shirt. Since then, Dad has mastered the basic rules of laundry: no red socks in with your whites, no tumble-drying somebody's favourite Tommy Hilfiger, no jamming the drainage hose with loose change.

'You know what I need?' Dad says.

'Go on, surprise me.'

'A life.'

'So what does that mean?' I ask.

Dad just shrugs but I know he's up to something.

'Why can't they design shirts better?' Dad moans, standing the iron up on the ironing board.

'How do you mean?'

'They're such weird shapes. Couldn't they make them more – well, regular?'

'They could,' I say. 'But you'd need cube-shaped people to wear them.'

Dad grins.

'I take your point.'

It's seven o'clock. Gary didn't come home for tea. Dad's trying not to sound concerned. I'm going along with the act. He pulls the next item out of the basket. It's a blouse. I do a double-take.

46

'Dad, that's Mum's!'

'Oh, don't kick off on me,' says Dad.

I will if you don't tell me why you've got it.

'So are you going to tell me what you're doing with it?' I ask, my stomach clenching.

'I'm taking her stuff down the charity shop.'

I can feel my insides turning over. It's like we're burying her all over again. Doesn't it ever end?

'Throwing it out? But it's Mum's.'

Dad goes on ironing, then folds the blouse and puts it in his bin bag.

'And somebody's going to get some benefit from it. She's gone, John.'

Is it that simple to you, Dad? She's gone?

I remember the early days. Letters would come with her name on them. It was just junk mail but we would line them up on the kitchen surface, as if she were going to come and pick them up. Stupid, I know, but we couldn't quite believe she wasn't coming back. Life didn't make sense without her. As long as her photograph stood on the sideboard, as long as her clothes hung in the wardrobe, she couldn't really be dead. I kept thinking it was all just a cruel, elaborate game. I wanted her back *so much*. Whenever something happened, I could hear what she would say about it, just as if she were right there next to me. When you know somebody inside out, when you know their every characteristic, their outlook on life down to the last detail, how can you tell yourself that you'll never see them again?

Disgusted at Dad's attitude, I turn for the door. Without looking back, I leave him with my parting shot.

'Gone? Don't you think I know that?'

Gary rolls in at twenty to eleven.

'I thought I told you to have your mobile on,' Dad snaps.

I'm back downstairs now, but we've barely spoken.

'The charger's broken,' Gary says, cool as you like.

'When did this happen?'

'Dunno. I only noticed it tonight.'

Convenient.

'So why didn't you come home and tell me?'

Dad's handling this all wrong, but after the ironing confrontation he's been building up to it all night. Mum was different. She didn't let things build up. That's the trouble with Dad, he allows things to slide for weeks then erupts.

'I told you to be in at ten!' he roars.

'Half past,' says Gary, correcting him. 'Ten o'clock on a schoolday, but it's Bank Holiday tomorrow.'

Dad starts to deflate like a rubber dinghy with the plug pulled out. Like I knew he would. He's nothing if not consistent.

'OK, half past—'

'There. I set off at half past so I'm on time really.'

Cocky get, our Gary. I find myself willing Dad to put him in his place.

'That's not the point. Your room's a mess . . .'

'Done. I'll tidy it tomorrow.'

Boy, do I feel let down. It's as if Dad's shrinking before my eyes. When did he become such a wuss? Stupid question, it was the day Mum died, wasn't it?

'You didn't come home for tea,' says Dad.

'I ate at Sean's.'

OK, Dad, so what's left in the armoury?

'I didn't know where you were.'

Is that it? You *are* feeble! Gary's bound to have an answer for that.

'I phoned you from Sean's but nobody picked up.'

Told you.

'You've got an answer for everything, haven't you?' Dad says in exasperation.

48

His anger is draining away. He's lost the argument.

'Pretty much,' says Gary. 'Anyway, I'm going to bed.'

When he walks past I smell cigarette smoke on him. Good job Dad didn't notice.

Gran and Grandad Ferguson turn up at half past nine next morning. They're Mum's parents so Dad is like a cat on hot bricks. He wants to make an impression, prove that he can raise their grandchildren. He wants to be a Superdad. When the doorbell rings everyone is up except Gary. Dad shepherds my grandparents into the living room then joins me in the kitchen.

'Make them a pot of tea, John,' he says. 'I'm going to rouse His Majesty.'

He checks that neither of my grandparents is listening.

'I ask you, half nine on a Bank Holiday? Haven't they ever heard of a lie-in?'

Grandad was in the army, Kenya, Aden, Ireland, so the answer is no. I reckon he gives the cockerel his early morning call. Dad climbs the stairs two at a time. A moment late I hear Gary grumbling then Dad shouting.

'I said NOW!'

The next minute he's walking into the living room, just behind me and the tea tray. He's all smiles.

'That lad of mine,' he says nervously. 'He doesn't half like his sleep.'

'You shouldn't encourage him,' says Grandad. 'That's the trouble with young people. No sense of self-discipline.'

Dad tells his cold-flannel-on-the-back story. Grandad isn't impressed. I think it's because he's heard it before. Dad used to be repetitive but he's all right now . . .

. . . all right now . . .

. . . all right now . . .

'Still doing well at school?' Gran asks.

'Mm.'

I can't manage a yes. I'm a bit anxious about my GCSEs next month.

'You've always been the brainy one,' says Gran. 'Good job Gary's got his looks.'

So what does that say about me? I'm not quite Quasimodo, you know. Yvette likes me. Pity Olivia doesn't.

'What about Gary?' says Grandad, sipping his tea. 'Still not doing much?'

Dad shakes his head.

'All he's bothered about is going out with his mates.'

'You should put your foot down,' says Grandad. 'My auld feller would have taken his belt to me for less.'

'I don't hold with capital punishment,' says Dad.

He means corporal punishment but nobody seems to notice.

'A young lad needs a firm hand,' says Grandad.

Dad is still trying to show how firm he is when Gary comes down. He's still only half-dressed.

'Haven't you even had a wash or brushed your teeth?' Dad asks despairingly.

'I'll do it in a minute,' Gary yawns.

'You'll do it now.'

Gary does his Harry Enfield teenager bit up the stairs and Dad asks Gran and Grandad about their holiday in Scotland.

The moment Gran and Grandad are gone, Gary shoots out of the house. This time I follow. I ride up Moss Lane and spot him outside Blockbuster Video. He's with Sean, Tony and Adrian. I think I've got a handle on this Adrian. I reckon he fancies himself as a bit of a Fagin, getting kids to do stuff for him, robbing maybe. I just hope I'm wrong.

After a few minutes, Sean and Tony detach themselves and head for the takeaway pizza. I crouch behind the wall. It soon becomes obvious that they're not interested in eating. They go inside and run out again a few seconds later, shouting abuse. The owner chases them with what looks like a snooker cue.

'You don't go near the till,' he shouts in an Italian accent. 'Young hoodlums.'

It sounds more like *young doodlebums*. I feel sick. Why do I have to be right all the time?

Sean and Tony don't retreat far. The moment the owner goes back inside they run up and spit on the window. Satisfied with their work, they return to Adrian and Gary. Adrian says something and they follow him to his car. They are pulling away when the owner of the pizza place comes out with a bowl of soapy water and starts washing his window.

Young doodlebums.

Gary is in spot on ten o'clock tonight. Dad is pleased but only for a couple of minutes. When Gary walks past him Dad wrinkles his nose.

'Are you smoking, Gary?' he asks.

'No way,' Gary protests, just a bit too strongly. 'It'll be off Adrian.'

'Who's Adrian?'

'Just a mate.'

Dad catches my eye. Needless to say, I look away.

4

The way things are at home, I really look forward to school, especially Olivia Bellman. Unfortunately, Yvette is on hand to make me feel guilty even about that pleasure.

'Adam was only kidding on Saturday, wasn't he?' she asks, catching me up. Her upper lip is curled self-consciously over her braced teeth. 'You can't be after Olivia.'

'Well,' I say, wishing Yvette could be happy for me, 'I do like her.'

'Oh John!'

'Why, what's the matter with her?'

Yvette shakes her head.

'Have you ever actually talked to her? She's a complete bimbo. You could say she's got hidden shallows.'

'Exactly what I've been saying,' Adam chips in. 'Only I didn't put it quite as well.'

I'm about to protest that bimbos aren't heading for ten GCSEs when Olivia, she of the golden tresses, puts in an appearance. Kedra gives Yvette one glance and announces: '*Brace* yourself for Maths everyone.'

Yvette's prehensile lip clings even more tightly to her front teeth. I detect a distinct quiver in her chin. Girls might not get into fights the same way lads do, but they can do just as much damage with those verbals.

'That was uncalled for,' says Adam.

I know it should have been me who stuck up for Yvette, but the moment's gone. I comfort myself with the thought that at least Olivia didn't say it.

Last lesson Tuesday afternoon is Drama. Mrs Owen comes in with a tall, blond guy in deck pumps.

'Who's the hippie?' whispers Adam.

'Not an inspector, that's for certain. What do you reckon, musician?'

'Artist?'

'This,' Mrs Owen says, 'is Brendan.'

First name terms, eh? Not an inspector then. Adam and I exchange glances.

'Actor.'

'Brendan,' Mrs Owens tells us, 'is part of Trapdoor Theatre Company.'

Adam and I exchange high fives.

'Brendan is going to be working with us for the next six weeks on *Romeo and Juliet*.'

Olivia's hand shoots up.

'But it's our GCSEs!'

'Yes, and *Romeo and Juliet* is a set text. The work we do with Brendan will give us an extra insight.'

'It does seem a bit much,' I say, keen to earn some Brownie points with Olivia.

Olivia just ignores me.

'Well, I think it's a great idea,' Yvette declares. 'We need something different, something creative. All we ever do is revise, revise, revise.'

Mrs Owen nods approvingly. She's one of your education-for-life types.

'OK,' says Mrs Owen. 'We've had our little slice of democracy. The bottom line, people, is this: the next six weeks' work on *Romeo and Juliet* counts towards your exam. We're doing it, end of story.'

She stares Olivia down.

'Right, over to you, Brendan.'

The girls seem to like Brendan. He's kind of Brad

Pitt-ish in a downmarket kind of way. The rest of us are happy to be doing something different, so we lend Brendan our ears.

'Doing *Romeo and Juliet* I can understand,' I say. 'Performing it as part of the exams I get. But putting it on for the parents at the end of term? Isn't that a bit much?'

'Oh, just listen to Olivia Bellman's mouthpiece,' says Adam.

We make our way down the bus, trying to find a seat as far from the Year 7s as possible.

'John, it'll be a laugh.'

'Yes, but at whose expense? You're not Romeo.'

'Oh, stop whingeing. You've only got to learn a few scenes. It's not like we've got to perform the whole play.'

I look at the hand-out Brendan gave us: *Romeo and Juliet, snapshots of a passion*. Only my snapshots will be of Yvette, not Olivia. Bummer!

'Besides,' Adam says, 'if you didn't want to be Romeo why did you do the part so well?'

'Because,' I inform him, 'I thought Olivia would be Juliet. She always gets the female lead.'

'That's what comes of counting your chickens before they're hatched,' Adam says.

'I've a good mind to turn your chickens into rotten omelettes,' I tell him.

'Come again?'

'It sounded good in my head,' I say.

He nudges me in the ribs.

'Yvette, though, she'll make a lovely Juliet. Well, except for the braces, the freckles, the chubby cheeks and the fact that she's a midget.'

'Don't be so mean!'

Adam laughs like a horse.

'So you do have a soft spot for her after all! I knew it.'

Crafty sod. All I can say after that is, 'D'oh!'

To my surprise, Gary is in when I get home. Most days he is out of his uniform and out of the house before I walk through the door.

'I didn't expect to find you in,' I say.

He hands me a sheet of paper roughly torn from a notepad:

> *Gary,*
> *Be in when I get home.*
> *I want a word.*
> *Dad.*

'I wonder what the word is,' I say.

Dad's words are rarely positive. They usually begin with **Don't** and end with **you ever!**

'Did you blow me up?'

'You know me better than that.'

Gary nods.

'So what gives?'

'Maybe he's seen Mick's dad.'

Gary raises his eyes to the ceiling.

'Mick and his big mouth.'

'Don't go blaming Mick. He's the best friend you've ever had. You're the one who's taken up with the weird mates.'

'Why are they weird?'

'Do I have to spell it out?'

'Yes.'

'Well,' I begin. 'For starters, there's Sean Pike.'

'Sean's all right.'

'Yes, except he's got a psycho brother doing time in Walton jail.'

'That's Eddie, not Sean.'

'Got an answer for everything, haven't you? So what about Adrian?'

'What about him?'

'He's seventeen but he hangs around with a bunch of kids.'

'We're not kids. Besides, all his mates have joined the Army. His girlfriend is Sean's cousin. It just kind of happened.'

'Yes, and it's more than a bit odd.'

'You're the one that's odd, stuck in the house reading your stupid books. You don't have a life so you want to ruin mine.'

'What do you mean, I haven't got a life?'

Gary laughs.

'What do you do every night? Finish your homework then read or watch TV. You're a nerd.'

I refuse to sit back and take it. I give as good as I get.

'Loser!'

'Moron!'

'Billy No-mates!'

'Dweeb!'

This carries on until we run out of insults. Gary goes on the X box. Dr Dre blasts out of his room. I have my tea and do my homework, then return fire with Linkin Park. When the neighbours start knocking on the wall we both turn down the volume.

Dad hits the ground running the moment he comes through the door. Gary comes out on the landing to face the music.

'About turn, sunshine,' says Dad, charging upstairs like a superannuated SAS man.

Panic shows in Gary's eyes.

'Where are we going?'

'To your room.'

'I'll tidy it,' says Gary, in just a bit too much of a hurry to reach his bedroom door.

'Too right you will,' says Dad. 'But this isn't about tidying.'

'So what—?'

I watch them from across the landing. Dad marches past Gary into his room. I hear the cupboard doors under Gary's bed slide open. Dad returns with a small tin and three bottles of Vodka Ice. Full ones.

'Would you like to explain this lot?'

Gary's mouth falls open. Mine follows suit. Dad goes back for another look and comes back with four more bottles, empty this time.

'And this?'

More bottles.

'And this?'

Even more. That's some stash Gary's built up.

'You didn't think chucking a few sweaters over the top would disguise it, did you?' Dad asks. 'Credit me with *some* sense.'

'You had no right!' Gary whines. 'It's my room.'

'Gary,' says Dad, 'I'd think very carefully about what you say next.'

He picks up the tin.

'Now, what could this be, I wonder? Is this a cannabis sticker on the lid?'

'It's only a bit of weed,' Gary protests.

For a moment, I think Dad is shaping up to hit him. Some of the local estates have got major drugs problems. Mum and Dad have always been worried about us getting drawn in.

'Only! If you hadn't noticed, it's illegal!'

'Everybody uses it,' says Gary. 'Ask John.'

'Don't drag *me* into this,' I tell him.

'Even the coppers say it doesn't matter. Tobacco and alcohol are worse.'

'Gary, you're using cannabis *and* tobacco *and* alcohol.'

A hit, Dad, a palpable hit. Now don't go over the top.

'Are you *trying* to get in trouble with the police? Are you?'

'It's only for personal use.'

Ouch. Wrong thing to say, Gary.

'Where've you got this stuff from?' Dad asks. 'These new mates of yours?'

Calm down, Dad.

'There's too much here for one person. Who's been in your room helping you consume this little lot?'

Another question strikes him.

'And when did you have them round?'

Dad's eyes widen. The penny has dropped.

'You've been sagging school!'

'No, I haven't.'

Dad snatches Gary's blazer off the peg. He starts rummaging through the pockets. He finds two letters from school about unauthorised absences. Honestly, Gary's too dense even to dump the evidence.

'That does it, lad. You're grounded. Got that? Grounded!'

The hand holding the letters is trembling. Oh-oh! Going over the top . . .

'Do you think I want to end up with a crack-dealer for a son?'

Way over the top!

'Now you're being stupid,' says Gary. 'I don't do the hard stuff.'

Which is just about the worst thing he could say in the circumstances.

'Maybe not,' Dad says, 'but the way you're going it's just a matter of time, isn't it?'

'Dad,' says Gary. 'You're so full of—'

Dad grabs Gary by the shoulders. He chokes off the protest and starts shaking him like a rag doll. So I'm looking at the pair of them, two kamikaze pilots heading for the same ship.

'What have I done to deserve this, you little—?'

As he shouts he is spraying Gary's face with spittle. It's time I stepped in.

'Dad!'

There, I've stepped in. Dad unhands Gary and steps back panting.

'Tidy—that—room,' he wheezes. 'It'll give you something to do while you're grounded.'

'This isn't fair,' Gary protests, almost in tears. 'Not fair.'

'Aw, diddums,' Dad snarls back. 'Life isn't fair, son. If it was, I wouldn't be a widower and you wouldn't be a liability.'

Under protest, Gary sets about tidying his room. Dad throws the bottles in a bin bag.

'Mum wouldn't act this way,' Gary says, just a bit too loud.

Dad's head snaps round.

'What did you say?'

He hurls the bin bags against the wall. The glass bottles shatter. As Dad advances Gary retreats. His hands go up in self-defence. He raises one knee, too, which would look funny if the whole thing weren't so out of hand.

'Oh, don't worry,' says Dad. 'I'm not going to touch you, but don't you *ever* try to use your mother against me. If Lisa saw the way you're turning out, she'd be ashamed.'

He turns and stamps downstairs. Now Gary is crying.

'Ashamed!' Dad yells from the bottom of the stairs.

It's only when I retreat to my room and feel the cold on my cheeks that I realise: I'm crying too.

5

Three days into his grounding, Gary is sticking to the rules. He's home every day by a quarter to four and he swears he's been attending school. It's Thursday, and Dad has just arrived home after doing two hours' overtime. The old man is still hanging up his coat when the doo-doo hits the fan. Gary's seen the state the kitchen is in and for once has decided to be helpful, so he's taking a bag out to the bin.

'Not that one,' Dad tells him.

'Why?' Gary asks. 'What's in it?'

Dad's face gives a twitch.

'Stuff for the charity shop,' he says.

But the blood drains from Gary's face when he looks inside.

'These are Mum's clothes!'

'That's right,' says Dad. 'I'm giving them to somebody who could make use of them. In case you haven't noticed, none of us are into cross-dressing.'

Way to go, Dad. Handled with all the sensitivity of a rampaging gorilla.

'But this is all that's left of Mum's,' Gary says, horrified.

Belatedly, Dad softens his tone. Even he can sense pain.

'Look, Gary, lad. We can't make the house a shrine to Lisa. Somebody will be glad of this.'

'So you're just going to throw her away like a pile of junk?' cries Gary.

'You can be one thoughtless little sod!' Dad shouts back. 'Lisa wasn't just *your mum*. She was *my wife*. I sit here for hours sometimes just looking through our photos or watching the family videos. That's what memories are made of. These are just clothes.'

Wrong thing to say. They're not just clothes, Dad, they're what's left over after a beautiful life has ended. Just like the photos and videos, these are a handle on the best person any of us ever knew. There's no such thing as *just* clothes, *just* perfume, *just* ornaments, not when they've been touched by somebody's life, by Mum.

Gary heads for the door.

'Where do you think you're going?' Dad asks.

'Out.'

Dad intercepts him. His eyes are blazing.

'Oh, no you don't. In case you've forgotten, you're still grounded.'

'I don't have to listen to you,' Gary retorts.

That's when Dad takes hold of him and swings him round. He does it with such force that Gary cannons into the hall door. He winces with pain and just when it looks like Dad is going to follow up with a slap, I make a grab for his arm. Dad's elbow catches me full in the face. Before I know it, blood is pouring from my nose.

'John! I'm sorry, son. I didn't see you coming.'

'Oh,' says Gary. 'So it's all right to smack me around but if you hit John it's a big tragedy.'

'I didn't smack you around!' Dad yells.

Which is the moment Adam chooses to ring the door-bell. Dad opens the door.

'Yes?'

Adam just stands staring and says, 'Have I come at a bad time?'

A little while later, it's calmer: I've brokered a unilateral cease-fire. Gary is in his room playing *Metal Gear Solid*. I'm at the kitchen table with cotton wool sticking out of both nostrils. Dad is in the living room watching *East-Enders*. Mum got him into it. I think he watches it because it reminds him of her. It's a bit like the way he still makes coffee for two sometimes, then stands looking at the cups for minutes on end.

'Do you do this often?' Adam asks.

'It's getting more frequent,' I say, ruefully.

God, my nose hurts. I inspect it in the mirror.

'So, what triggered World War Three?'

I explain about Mum's clothes.

'Doesn't take much to set Gary off, does it?'

I say nothing. I'm with Gary on this one. I tell Adam about the booze and Gary's 'bit of weed'.

'It's not that big a deal though, is it?' says Adam. 'We smuggled some cider up to your room once.'

'Ssh! Dad doesn't know about that. It's not just today. Gary's losing it.'

'So you don't think this'll be the end of it?'

'No,' I answer. 'Not by a long chalk.'

It's Saturday, the last day of Gary's grounding. Knowing Gary won't want to endanger his freedom, Dad picks today to spring a surprise.

'I'm going on another date,' he announces.

'Who with?' I ask, surprised.

'Her name's Rose.'

By way of a wordless protest, Gary stamps out of the room. I'd follow him, but it's not my style.

'So, how did you meet *this* one?' I ask, heavy on the disapproval.

Dad hears the acid in my voice and sighs.

'I *haven't* met her yet,' he says.

'OK,' I say. 'Now you've lost me.'

Dad stares at the tips of his shoes.

'I used a dating agency.'

'You what?'

Now this really does smack of desperation.

'Don't sound so shocked,' he says.

That wasn't shocked, I want to tell him, that was disgusted. It's time you knew the difference.

'Hang on a minute,' I say. 'What about Gary?'

'What about Gary?'

'He's grounded. I hope you're not expecting me to keep an eye on him for you?'

'I won't be gone long, just this afternoon.'

Yes, and imagine what could happen in an afternoon.

'But what if Gary does something?' I complain. 'This isn't fair!'

'I won't be long, son. We're going to Chester Zoo.'

Chester Zoo! What is she, a penguin?

'Come on,' Dad says. 'You're OK with this, aren't you?'

I grunt my protest.

'Looks like I've got to be.'

The bell rings at about three o'clock. Gary beats me to the door. It's Sean and Tony. No Adrian, thank God. I've still got this picture in my head, Adrian as Fagin and our Gary as the Artful Dodger.

'You can't go out!' I yell.

'What's it to you?'

'You heard what Dad said. No mates round and no going out. You're grounded until tomorrow.'

'You know the old saying,' Gary says. 'What the eye doesn't see, the heart doesn't grieve over.'

'But you're dropping me in it! Dad put me in charge.'

'Well, sorry, boss,' says Gary, winking to his mates. 'But tough. It's not like you're going to say anything, is it?'

With a sinking heart I watch Gary's mates troop in. They go upstairs. For the next fifteen minutes I'm so tense I can't get on with anything.

When Gary finally shows them to the door, I overhear him saying, 'Noon it is then. See you tomorrow.'

Dad rolls in just after six. I've decided to ignore him, but it's hard when he goes slamming cupboards and banging stuff about.

'OK?' I ask. 'How did it go?'

'You don't want to know.'

True. I don't. But we've gone this far.

'Yes,' I say firmly. 'I do.'

'She grabbed me in the fruit bats.'

Up till now, I really *didn't* want to know, but now I'm hooked.

'I beg your pardon!'

'In the Twilight Zone, the bat house, she made a lunge for me.'

Sounds a bit over the top. Who does Dad think he is, George Clooney?

'Are you sure about this?'

'John, I know when a woman's got hold of me.'

'Where?'

'I told you, in the fruit bats.'

'No, I mean where on your person did she grab you?'

'Oh,' says Dad. 'I'd rather not say.'

'So, it wasn't a success?'

'Hardly,' says Dad. 'Then, to top it all, a llama spat on my ice cream.'

'Magnum?'

'I don't know what kind of llama it was.'

'No, the ice cream, was it a Magnum?'

'Oh,' says Dad. 'You mean you want one.'

I didn't actually, but I do now.

'Yes, I'll go to the shop. Do you want anything?'

Dad puts in his order. Anything with chocolate. I take Gary's order and head for the door.

'By the way,' Dad calls, 'has our Gary behaved himself?'

How do I field this one? I decide to plump for spineless dishonesty.

'Sure,' I answer. 'No problems.'

Adam and I are out on our bikes. Health-conscious, that's us, the sons of Enid Blyton. Cycling, sunshine and lashings of ginger beer. OK, so we're stalking Olivia. Not as wholesome as a picnic in the country but a lot more fun. Adam's found out that she goes to this tennis club down the south end. As luck would have it, the cross-city cycle path goes right past it.

'Where do you get your information?' I ask.

Adam taps the side of his nose.

'Wouldn't you like to know?'

'Yes, that's why I asked.'

'Well, I'm not telling. It's a secret.'

'It's Yvette, isn't it?'

'Give over,' says Adam. 'She's not going to help you cop off with the delicious Ms Bellman, is she?'

'Maybe not.'

'There's no "maybe" about it. She'd chew her own leg off first. Come to think of it, those braces would help.'

'You can cut out the braces jokes,' I tell him.

'Touchy,' says Adam. 'Who's got a soft spot for Yvette then?'

'Behave. She's a mate. I don't think of her like that.'

'I think of every girl like that.'

'Well, I don't. Me and Yvette, it's purely platonic.'

'We'll see,' says Adam. 'We'll see.'

Not only does the cycle path go close to the tennis club, it overlooks it. And guess who's playing right by the fence? Got it in one: Olivia. She's playing Kedra. I watch her move across the court, fluid and athletic. She's wearing a dazzling white tennis skirt and top. It's so white it seems to flash against her tanned arms and legs.

'She didn't get *that* tan out of a bottle,' I observe.

'No,' says Adam, a mine of information as always. 'The family has got a villa in the Algarve. They top up their tan two or three times a year.'

I gaze longingly at Olivia. Villa in the Algarve! All we've ever managed is a caravan in Talacre!

'John,' says Adam, 'close your mouth. Your tongue's hanging out.'

But I keep on looking at Olivia. So that's how the other half live. I bet she didn't turn up for her interview at St Thomas's in a two-tone Frankenstein car, courtesy of Dessie's Scrapyard. A villa in the Algarve! I can just see myself rubbing Factor 30 on her back and shoulders.

'They're good, aren't they?' says Adam.

We're edging closer to the embankment that overlooks the courts. The rally ends when Olivia hits the ball into the net.

'Stupid lace!' she snaps, bending down to secure her shoes.

'There's nothing wrong with her laces,' says Adam. 'She's just a bad loser.'

I'm not listening. From here I can see down her top. My heart's going thump-a-dump. My hands go clammy. My brain's calling me a sexist bum but the rest of me is saying: *who cares?* Then my whole world starts slipping away. Hang on, my whole world *is* slipping away. I'm too close to the edge. Suddenly I'm tumbling head-over-heels down the embankment. My bike is somersaulting over me. Dust smears me, chippings cut me, thistles scratch me and nettles sting me. I'm in a seriously embarrassing serves-you-right-for-leching situation.

'Ow, ow, ow!'

I'm doing my imitation of Homer Simpson tumbling

down Springfield Gorge. I end up crashing into the fence twisted into the shape of a pretzel with my bike on top of me. Olivia gives me the kind of look you reserve for a squashed cockroach.

'Oh, hi Olivia,' I say, bike oil trickling down my cheek. 'Fancy bumping into you here.'

She spins on her heel and marches away, ponytail bobbing.

'Creep,' she says.

'How do I explain that away?' I groan.

My dreams of summer evenings with Olivia are popping like so many party balloons.

'You don't,' says Adam. 'Just tell her the truth: you want to be her love-slave.'

'Thanks for nothing.'

We're crossing Rice Lane when we spot Gary. He's helping Tony, Sean and Adrian push Adrian's car. There's a girl in the front seat steering. Must be the girlfriend.

'What gives, Gaz?' I ask. 'Elastic band gone?'

'Clear off,' says Adrian.

It's the first time I've had a real good look at him. He seems a nasty piece of work.

Hard face. Cold eyes.

'I can smell petrol,' says Adam.

'Hardly surprising,' Sean explains. 'The petrol tank fell off.'

'A petrol tank can't just fall off,' Adam says, laughing.

'Well, this one did,' Tony says.

I peer underneath the car. Sure enough there are the tank and fuel pipe dragging along the road.

'Isn't this a bit dangerous?' I ask. 'I mean, one spark and the whole lot could go up in flames.'

Just think what Dad would say if he knew Gary had been riding round in this death-trap.

67

'How did it get through its MOT?'

Adrian eyeballs me. I get the feeling it's a while since this jalopy saw the inside of a garage. Legal it ain't.

'Do one,' he says.

Adam is willing me to go.

'See you back home,' I say to Gary. 'Told you cycling was quicker than driving.'

I get the feeling I'm trying Adrian's patience. I finally take the hint and go.

Gary gets in at five to ten.

'What's this?' Dad says. 'Mr Stop-out five minutes early.'

'I'll go out again if you like,' Gary says.

Hell's teeth, Gary. Can't you make an effort? Just once?

'No need for that,' Dad tells him. 'I'm just glad you're sticking to the rules.'

He's trying to build bridges. Gary isn't interested.

'I'm turning in,' he says.

As he goes past I get a whiff of cigarette smoke and stale beer. Dad must have noticed but he's keeping quiet about it. I go up myself an hour later. Gary's light is on. I decide to have it out with him.

'You'd better not be smoking weed again,' I say.

'What's it to you?'

'You want to know?' I say, shoving my face into his. 'The way you behave is making us all miserable. Why do I have to suffer for a loser like you? Tell me that.'

Gary goes to speak, but I cut him short. I've had it with the grief he's giving this family. I've got all this resentment coiled in my stomach. It's time I got it out.

'And what's the score with Adrian's car?' I ask. 'It looks like a death-trap.'

'Nothing to worry about there, big brother,' says Gary with a sneer in his voice. 'He's scrapping it.'

That's something. At least Gaz won't be driving round in Adrian's iffy motor. I may have screwed up my chances with Olivia, but at least Gary's wings have been clipped. That's got to be good news.

Hasn't it?

6

On my way into school I'm stopped by Paul Martindale. I search my memory banks:

Martindale, Paul.
Upper Sixth.
Captain, St Thomas's rugby team.
Built like brick hithouse.

I scan for reasons why he might have a homicidal glint in his spooky blue eyes.

Search complete:
No matches found.

So why am I standing here like David without a sling-shot? What have I done to upset this apprentice Goliath?

'Listen here, weirdo,' he growls. 'You're getting on Olivia's nerves.'

Ah, so *that's* what I've done.

'And you're—?'

Not her boyfriend.

'Olivia's boyfriend.'

D'oh!

'I see.'

'You'd better, because if I ever catch you near her again, do you know what I'll do?'

'Er, no.'

'I'll extract your liver and, believe me, I won't use any anaesthetic to do it.'

For a moment, I imagine myself as Jean-Claude Van Damme. I pound this baboon to a pulp then turn to a passer-by, '*Sweep up that trash*,'.

Back in the real world I prefer to grovel.

'No need for that, Paul. I was only—'

'Shut up.'

Show him what you're made of, says Jean-Claude. Unfortunately, the stuff I'm made of is yellow and runny and you pour it on puddings. Look, Paul, this is me shutting up.

Z–z–z–ip.

'OK.'

He jabs his finger in my face. 'Olivia's with me. Got it?'

'Yes,' I say. 'Got it.'

Adam arrives just as Paul is going.

'What was that about?'

'My liver.'

'Come again?'

'You know, whether I wanted it surgically removed.'

'So what's Paul Martindale got against you?'

'I've been stalking his girlfriend.'

'What, you mean him and Olivia?'

I nod.

'This is bad.'

'Yes,' I say. 'Bad.'

Adam looks like a puppy who's just lost his favourite chewing slipper.

'Hang on,' I say. 'Am I missing something here? I'm the one who's had the death-threat. Why are you so miserable?'

Adam tries to cover himself.

'You know me, Mr Empathy. I'm showing solidarity with my love-lorn, brother-in-arms.'

I frown. He's hiding something.

For the rest of the morning, I avoid Olivia. I'm not going to cross Paul. Besotted I may be, stupid I am not. I get through the a.m. without upsetting King Kong's kid brother. Just the p.m. to go. Maths and Drama. Adam joins me in the dinner queue.

'Olivia history then?'

'No way.'

'But Paul—'

'But Paul nothing. I'll wait for the dust to settle and see how things pan out.'

Adam shakes his head.

'This lobotomy,' he says. 'Did you have to go private?'

'Look,' I say. 'It's an infatuation, an older-guy thing. Girls go through that. It won't last.'

'Where'd you get that?' Adam asks. 'Some American High School movie?'

I stare glumly at the gravy congealing round my chips.

'Yeah, how'd you know?'

Maths is just starting when I notice that Yvette is absent.

'Seen Yvette?' I ask Ros Thompson, her best friend.

'Orthodontist's. Adjustments to her braces.'

The mention of the word 'braces' attracts the Paradise Set.

'You wouldn't catch me wearing braces,' says Philippa Blake. 'They make you look like Hannibal Lecter.'

'I know,' Gillian chimes in. 'Poor Yvette. Braces *and* freckles.'

Ros pulls a face. Adam watches the Paradise Set take their places.

'How do they do it?' he wonders out loud. 'How do they creep up like that?'

Ros shrugs.

'Dunno,' she says. 'But it's a wonder they don't leave slime trails.'

'Bummer about Yvette,' I say, remembering it's Drama next. 'How do we do *Romeo and Juliet* without a Juliet?'

'Easy,' says Adam. 'The understudy.'

We think for a moment then chorus, 'Olivia!'

'But what if the Incredible Bulk finds out?' I groan.

'Then you fight him,' says Adam with a grin. 'I'll hold your coat.'

Mr Walker is explaining that Pythagoras's Theorem goes hand in hand with Sin, Cos and *Tan*. All I can think about is Paul Martindale. He goes hand in hand with pain, hurt and death.

'I can't fight him,' I whisper. 'He'll eat me alive. I'm too young to die.'

'Do you think we could keep our minds on right-angled triangles?' Mr Walker says, eyeballing us. 'I think that's the sound of approaching exams I hear in the distance.'

The only sound I can hear is that of John Cain in traction!

'OK,' says Brendan. 'Where's Mercutio?'

Adam steps forward.

'And Romeo?'

I'm stealing glances at Olivia. Any moment now I get to kiss her. Talk about 'sweet sorrow'! One kiss. Price: a merciless pounding courtesy of Paul Martindale. Adam is rambling through his lines but I don't pay much attention. My mind is on two things and two things only: Olivia's lips and Paul's fists. Or is that four things? How did I get myself into this?

'Romeo. *Romeo!*'

Brendan is staring at me, willing me to say my lines.

'Oh yes, right.'

So I bolt through them, ending: '*On lusty gentlemen.*'

I can't help stealing a look at Olivia. She twists her face

in disgust. I don't think I'm her favourite lusty gentleman right now.

This is it. Tybalt's just about done working himself up into a steaming rage about Romeo's appearance. Now it's just Olivia and I. The love scene. I think of Paul Martindale, the big, humourless lump. Is Olivia worth the aggro I'm bringing on myself? I look at her: long, blonde hair falling straight and silky down her back and reaching almost to her waist; shapely legs; full, slightly-parted lips. We're talking Aphrodite in a clam! Of course she's worth it. I'm actually going to do this. I'm going to kiss Olivia Bellman.

'Right, then,' says Brendan. 'Romeo, Juliet, this is it, the lead-in to the first kiss. So let's crank up the passion.'

I can hear the Paradise Set sniggering behind their hands. Who cares? Olivia's lips are waiting.

'*My lips, two blushing pilgrims, ready stand,*' I read.

Oh, they're standing ready all right. I could hug Yvette's orthodontist for this.

Because of the brace adjustments I'm about to kiss Olivia.

'*Thus from my lips,*' I say, hardly able to breathe. '*By thine my sin is purg'd.*'

I lean forward only to hear Brendan's hands clap together. The sound hits my ear like a door closing. Olivia turns to look at Brendan and my nose brushes her ear before finally coming to rest in her hair.

'Yew!' she protests. 'What did you just do, wipe your nose on my hair?'

'No,' I cry, mortified. 'I thought—'

More giggles from the Paradise Set.

'Thought what?'

'Dunno.'

I retreat in disarray. Little bits of me lie dead on the field of battle. Only Adam understands the agony I'm suffering. Great, it looks like I get the pounding *without* the kiss.

I'm out of the Drama department like a cork from a champagne bottle.

'That was *so* embarrassing!' I groan.

'Didn't you hear Brendan?' Adam asks.

'No.'

'He said we'd leave the kiss until Yvette got back. It was good when you wiped your nose on Olivia's hair, though,' chuckles Adam. 'Nice touch.'

Then Paul puts in an appearance.

'Uh oh.'

He is bearing down on me. Look at the big, dumb baboon. What does she see in him? OK, so he's got chiselled good looks. Yes, and muscles like grapefruit in a bag. Oh, and he's grown out of his spots. Then there's the car his dad bought him. But, other than the good looks, the muscles, the spotlessness and the car, what's he got going for him?

I start to take a step back but I've no need to worry. He isn't after me. He sweeps past.

I turn to see Olivia run up to him and kiss him.

'That's disgusting!' I say. 'On school grounds, too.'

'It wouldn't be disgusting if you were doing it, would it?' Adam says.

No. It would be wonderful.

7

I have to push my way through a small crowd to get into the house. It isn't just the usual suspects: Sean and Tony. There are a couple of girls with them. They're not bad-looking either. Don't tell me Gary's pulled! It's supposed to be the other way round. The big brother does the dating.

'Are you going out?' I ask.

The two girls are munching chewing gum and looking me up and down. I'm feeling self-conscious.

'Might be,' Gary says.

That's as much as I get out of him. Most of the time, Gary talks in grunts. Sean, Tony and the girls are smoking. I take a deep breath and hurry inside. I've hated the rancid smell of cigarette smoke for as long as I can remember. How can anything that disgusting be considered cool? Hey, look at me, I stink and I'm giving myself cancer. Cool, huh? If Olivia started smoking I'd drop her like a lump of red hot metal. Well, maybe not.

I get as far as the kitchen door when curiosity gets the better of me. I sneak into the living room and peek through the net curtains. The two girls really are something, even if they do chew gum and smoke cigarettes. They can't be with Gary. I'm still looking when one of them spots me. She pulls tongues and laughs like I'm the world's funniest joke. I shrink back. Suddenly, everyone is laughing at me. I'm retreating down the hall when I hear Gary joining in, 'John? You're not kidding. What a prat.'

Smarting from my prattishness, I search the fridge for something to eat.

Complete list of contents:

* two ounces of Cheddar cheese, gone hard and cracked because it isn't wrapped;

* similar amount of Cheshire cheese, speckled with blue mould (bleuch!);

* one tortilla, curling up;

* enough milk swilling round the bottom of a two litre carton to fill an egg cup;

* one sachet of black bean sauce;

* one Scotch egg;

* one tub of spreadable butter.

I open the bread bin. Complete list of contents:

* three rounds of bread, dry but not yet mouldy;

* one crumpet;

* three cashew nuts, ready salted;

* one ant (black).

For tea, I end up eating three rounds of toast, one crumpet, three cashew nuts and half a Scotch egg. I throw the other half away. (So that's where the ant went!) I wash it down with the milk, then gag: it's gone sour. I'm in the bathroom trying to rinse away the taste with mouthwash when the front door goes.

'Gary?'

'No, it's me, Dad. Gary's out, I assume.'

'Yes.'

'By the way,' Dad says. 'I've just been shopping. Don't drink the milk in the fridge. It's on the turn.'

I give my mouth a third rinse.

'Too late.'

Dad asks me to take a video back. I think about taking my bike then remember Gary getting his nicked from outside the shop last January. So I walk instead. I'm just passing the pizza place, remembering the spit on the window, when I hear a car gunning down the road. It's a blue Nissan and it must be doing at least sixty. I catch sight of the driver. It's Adrian. The car speeds out of sight past the Bingo Hall. So where did Adrian get the new car? I'm sure Gary said he couldn't afford a new one. I walk into the video shop feeling uneasy.

So many questions.

So few answers.

It's half past ten when Gary rolls in. I hear a car pulling away. Suddenly, I wonder if it's a blue Nissan.

'I thought I said ten o'clock on a school day,' Dad grumbles.

For the last half hour he's been up and down like a yo-yo.

'Well, you're in early tomorrow.'

'How early?'

'You're half an hour late so I want you in half an hour early tomorrow night.'

Gary relaxes. He knows he's getting off easy.

'Are you sure I can't have until ten?' he asks. 'I'll make sure I'm on time.'

Talk about pushing it! I look at Dad. You're never falling for it.

'Half past nine,' Dad tells him.

Dad gives me a look that says: that put him in his place.

Gary immediately gives me one that says: I can twist the old man round my little finger.

Guess who's closer to the truth.

Another Tuesday. We start with English, which is mostly revision. Then it's History, revision again. Then ICT which is also revision. For dinner we have a mild, Sainsbury-ish curry. This isn't revision, it's food, something we don't seem to get at home any more. Remembering the sour milk episode, I thank my lucky stars for school dinners. I never thought I'd say that!

In the afternoon, it's French, which is revision, followed by Science revision. The day ends with our form tutor stressing the importance of revision!

Just to add to the feeling of *déjà vu*, Olivia starts the day ignoring me, overlooks me all morning, fails to make eye contact during the dinner hour and forgets I exist all afternoon. At home time, just in case I haven't got the message, she cuts me dead at the bus stop.

If anybody asks how my day has been I will scream.

'How's your day been?' Gary asks when I get home.

I don't scream: I'm too surprised. I can't remember the last time we exchanged a civil word.

'OK,' I say.

I'm not having Gary thinking I'm a loser.

'I had a lousy day,' he says.

I don't believe this. He's actually talking to me!

'Why, what happened?'

'I had a run-in with my Maths teacher.'

Oh crap! So that's why he's talking to me. He's got himself in trouble again. Once Dad finds out the fur is going to fly. I once said I'd be there for Gary. It seemed quite heroic at the time. The reality is different. It's grubby and nasty and I don't want to do it any more. Why can't somebody be there for me for once? Why've I got to shoulder all the burden? I take a deep breath.

'What sort of run-in?'

'The sort that gets you one of these.'

He hands me a letter addressed to Dad. I feel sick. The weird thing about Gary getting in trouble is that I'm the one who feels guilty!

'Oh, that sort.'

'I can't just hide it, either. There's a tear-off slip I have to return.'

He gives me a sidelong look.

'You couldn't sign it, could you? Your handwriting could pass for an adult's.'

As opposed to Gary's, which might pass for a monkey's.

'So that's it!'

I feel cheated. I knew it. He wasn't being nice. He was using me again. What is it with me? Have I got something written on my face?

'*Welcome mat – walk on me.*'

My frustration comes spitting out.

'For a minute there, you had me fooled, Gaz. I actually thought you wanted to talk. Shows what a mug I am. All you wanted was for me to forge Dad's signature.'

'But he'll go ape when he reads this,' Gary says.

'You should have thought about that before—What *did* you do anyway?'

'I don't know. Walshy was getting on my nerves.'

'So you—?'

Gary looks at the floor.

'I threw a text book at him.'

'Oh, way to go Gary! That was clever.'

'I hate school,' he says. 'It's boring and all they ever do is shout.'

I'm not in the mood for his whining.

'I see,' I retort, 'and nothing's ever your fault, is it? You know what, Gary, this time you're on your own. Sort out your own mess. Either that or you're heading for big trouble.'

'Oh, here we go again,' says Gary. 'You're my brother, John, not my mum. Just because you haven't got a life.'

'And you have, I suppose?'

'Meaning?'

'Hanging round on street corners, smoking weed, getting

drunk, dropping stuff off the railway bridge, driving round in robbed cars. Sure, Gary, I'm really jealous.'

That last item is guesswork. Judging by the look on Gary's face, I'm not far from the mark. My sarcasm falls away. Now I'm scared and angry in equal parts.

'Oh, Gary, you moron! Tell me it wasn't robbed.'

He tries to recover.

'Don't be stupid.'

'Gary,' I say, 'look me in the eye and tell me that Nissan of Adrian's isn't stolen.'

Gary tries to go, but I block his way. I throw him back against the wall.

'You don't move till I get a straight answer. Is Adrian into joyriding?'

When Gary calls my bluff and refuses to answer, I shake my head and walk away.

'You're on your own, Gaz. I hope Dad grounds you for good.'

An hour later, Dad has just finished reading the letter.

'Why did you do it, Gary?' he says. 'You're not some two-bit scally. You've assaulted a teacher, for crying out loud!'

'I didn't assault him. I threw a book at him.'

'Dad throws his head back.

'And there's a difference?'

'I lost it, OK? I didn't mean to. It just sort of builds up, then I blow.'

'Well, next time try counting to ten.'

Gary shakes his head and looks away. That just sets Dad off again.

'Don't shake your head at me, lad!'

I'm wondering if this is Dad setting an example in counting to ten.

'I didn't—'

'Didn't you? *Didn't you?* Well, I say you did.'

'Fine,' says Gary. 'Have it your way.'

Gary is still looking away.

'Look at me, will you?' Dad yells, losing it completely.

Gary looks. His eyes are hard with frustration.

'For this,' Dad says, waving the letter, 'you're grounded for the rest of the week.'

'You've got to be joking!' Gary cries.

'Gary, you're grounded,' Dad retorts. 'Go to your room.'

Later that evening, Dad is out the back, hanging the clothes over the bars in the wash-house. Goodness knows why, but I'm actually feeling sorry for Gary.

'Dad only loses his temper because he cares,' I say.

'He's got a funny way of showing it,' Gary replies. 'He's just like the teachers. Shout, shout, shout.'

'He wants you to stay out of trouble, Gaz, that's all. Mum would have been just the same.'

I see the mask. He wants to shut out feelings he doesn't like.

'Don't bring Mum into this,' he says.

'Why not? She'd have died, seeing you like this.'

I wince at my choice of words. I try to recover.

'What I mean is—'

'John, I know exactly what you mean.'

His voice is flat. He's gone back behind the barricades. He hits me with everything he's got.

'You're making Mum die twice,' he says. 'That drunk driver killed her when he crashed his car into hers, but he was a stranger. You're family. What you and Dad are doing is worse.'

I stare at him in disbelief. I can't believe how hard and bitter he is. But by then I'm hardly thinking. I ball my fists like I want to smash them into Gary; beat down the walls of my lousy life. And he hasn't finished yet.

'You're killing her memory,' he hisses.

This time he's gone too far. What makes him think he's the only one hurting? All the times I've covered for him, all the lying I've done, all the crap I've had to put up with. Any shred of sympathy I've ever felt is turned into pure rage. I'm not interested in sorting this out. I just want to break something, and Gary will do.

'And what do you think you're doing to keep it alive?' I yell, my spit hitting his face. 'You know what you're doing?'

Every ounce of helpless bitterness and anger I've felt these last eleven months comes boiling out of me. Suddenly Gary isn't my brother. He's every rotten thing that's wrecked my life. He's the driver that killed my mum. He's the courts that failed to give us justice. He's the mess we're all in now.

'You,' I bawl, shoving my forefinger into his temple, 'you with your thieving and your druggy mates—'

It's all coming out, the fury, the despair.

'—you're spitting on her grave.'

The colour drops out of Gary's face. He almost runs from the room. It's only a few minutes later, when I've had time to think about what I said, that I start to regret it.

8

It's Wednesday, the second Drama lesson of the week. In school, they make a lesson out of Drama. Back home, we make a drama out of life.

'Big day,' says Adam, sucking on an extra-strong mint. 'You and Yvette. The big snog.'

He starts kissing his hand while making loud *mwa, mwa, mwa* noises. He's still snogging his hand when the Paradise Set glide by.

'Strange boy,' says Olivia.

Adam goes bright red for some reason I can't quite fathom. Since when did *he* care what the Paradise Set thought?

'It would be a bigger day if Olivia were Juliet,' I say glumly.

I'm expecting Adam to come back with a smart reply but he doesn't say a thing.

Curiouser and curiouser.

'Places everybody,' says Brendan.

Pretty soon, my lips are 'two blushing pilgrims' standing ready. Not quite as ready as they were on Monday, of course, but the lips they are standing ready for are Yvette's, not Olivia's. I take Yvette's hands and look into her eyes. I'm dying to laugh. This feels weird. I mean, we've been mates for eleven years. I used to yank her ponytails.

'. . . *let lips do what hands do!*'

Yvette's lips part slowly. Am I really going to kiss her? I once put a frog down her back. We were five.

'. . . *Thus from my lips*—'

I turn my head instinctively. Yvette does likewise. Are we doing this right? Whoever designed kissing couldn't have done any themselves!

'. . . *by thine my sin is purg'd.*'

I lower my face towards hers and that's quite a journey. I'd never quite realised how short she is! Maybe I should stand in a hole in the floor to even things up. Honestly, I could get backache doing this. I bend at the knees so I can lock onto her lips. I feel her breath on my mouth, the tender press of her lips. I smell a faint hint of perfume. Hey, what am I grumbling about? This isn't half bad. In the middle of the thrill of her kiss, I feel Yvette's hands touching my face. She's enjoying this as much as I am. Then her hands are pressing more firmly. Give over, that hurts!

That's when the panic sets in.

She isn't clinging to me in the grip of passion. She's trying to prise us apart. Now something's pinching. My lip, it's snagged on her braces somehow. Oh gross! *Oh cursed spite that ever I was trapped in Yvette's bite.* Ow! Now I think I'm bleeding. I see Brendan coming to help. No chance, buster, I can do this my own way. I yank myself free. Then the pair of us are blushing like traffic lights on stop. And I was right; when I touch my mouth there's a drop of blood.

'Next time,' Kedra says, 'we'll issue you with gum shields.'

Yvette turns and flees the room.

'Amazing how quickly she can run on those short legs,' says Olivia.

I stare at her. If there were a GCSE in cruelty she'd get an A star.

The house is empty when I get home, empty like the feeling

I get inside the moment I turn the corner of the street. It's getting so I hate the sight of the place. I look around. Thanks a bunch, Gary. Dad will crack up, and not just at you. Why can't you come straight home from school?

Hang on, the alarm is off. So where are you?

'Gary. Gaz?'

There's a breeze blowing through the house. The back door must be open.

'Gary?'

I can smell cigarette smoke. I push the door open just in time to see Sean and Tony disappearing in a haze through the back gate.

'You're not meant to have them round. You're still grounded.'

'So who's going to let on? You?'

'You shouldn't put this on me,' I protest.

There are three cigarette butts on the grass.

'And I thought you didn't smoke.'

'I don't.'

'*Three* butts.'

'So? One must be from another time.'

He's got an answer for everything, our Gary.

'You'd better get rid of them,' I say, 'or you'll be grounded for longer.'

'It's only smoking,' says Gary. 'It isn't even weed.'

'Just now, you daren't put a foot wrong,' I warn him.

He disposes of the evidence over the back fence.

'What do you see in those two?' I ask.

'They're mates.'

'Really?'

'I don't slag off Adam,' says Gary. 'What gives you the right to have a go at my mates?'

I shake my head and walk away. I look in the fridge. The cupboard is bare again. Dad could be done for neglect.

'Great,' I say. 'Absolutely flaming classic!'

'What's up?'

'Nothing for tea.'

'So, go the chippy.'

'No money.'

Gary pulls a ten pound note out of his pocket.

'Where'd you get this?' I ask suspiciously.

'Pocket money.'

'Since when did you save your pocket money?'

'Since I got grounded. I've nothing to spend it on stuck in this dump. Well, do you want it or not?'

My head says no but my stomach says yes.

'I'll take it. Do you want something from Pizza Reaction?'

'Thin crust ham and mushroom,' he says. 'Do you want to share a garlic bread?'

'Go on,' I say. 'Let's have a blow out.'

Gary and I are just finishing our pizza when Dad comes in. He looks tired.

'You OK?' I ask.

'Fine. It's all the overtime.'

'How come?'

'The plant's on a shutdown. We've got to get all the cleaning and maintenance done in a week. Any of that pizza left?'

'Sorry.'

He examines the fridge.

'Looks like I'm going straight out to the supermarket,' he says. 'Wonderful, you graft all day and you're not finished when you get in.'

I'm thinking, Mum never whinged about the shopping. She just got on with it. To my amazement, Gary offers to help.

'Let me go,' he says. 'I'll get the bus down and bring the shopping home in a taxi.'

But Dad isn't in the mood to accept.

'Forget it,' he says sourly. 'You're grounded.'

'I was only trying to help.'

'Well don't,' says Dad, shooting out a withering stare. 'I don't need your help.'

Gary looks crushed. For once, I don't think this was a manoeuvre. It was genuine, which doesn't mean anything to Dad. He's tired and he's fed up and Gary's as good a target for his frustrations as anybody.

'I know your game, lad. You just want to see your scally mates.'

Then he hits Gary with a low blow.

'I bet I wouldn't get all the shopping money back, either.'

He's only talking this way because he's tired but it's a horrible thing to say. The moment he says it he looks like he wants to take it back but the damage is done.

'You never trust me!' yells Gary.

Dad might be having second thoughts about the way he's handled Gary's offer, but he isn't about to back down.

'I wonder why.'

Gary gives Dad a hard stare and stamps up to his room. I shake my head.

'That went well.'

I help Dad put the shopping away when he gets in from the supermarket. Gary stays in his room. The sound of Shaggy booms across the landing.

'Think I should build bridges?' Dad asks.

'You!' I say. 'I'd leave well alone.'

Dad nods and loads the freezer.

'I got those lolly ices he likes,' he says. 'Peace offering.'

'Leave it,' I say. 'Let me speak to him. You get your tea.'

I go up to Gary's room. He's sitting on the floor with his back to me. I'm about to say something when I see the

88

bundle of notes in his hands. There are at least five tenners, maybe even double that.

'Where did you get that?'

Gary stuffs it hurriedly in his pocket.

'I told you, pocket money.'

'I wasn't born yesterday,' I tell him. 'Dad isn't that generous, and you're not that good at saving. Does this have something to do with Adrian?'

'Change the record, will you? That's all you ever say.'

'Gary, what are you getting yourself into?'

'Nothing. I told you, I've been saving my pocket money.'

'Yes, and next door's dog's gone veggie.'

'You're just the same as Dad,' Gary says. 'You always think the worst of me.'

After our last run-in, I don't plan to rise to the bait. I bite my tongue and walk out.

Five minutes later, I'm sitting in my room in the fading light wondering about the money. No matter how much I turn it over in my mind, I can only come up with one conclusion: Gary's getting himself in deep water.

It's hours before I go to sleep that night. I just lie there watching all the crap in my life come seeping out of the corners of the room. It's like I'm living every day on a sheet of ice. From all four corners hairline cracks are spreading. Jeez, look at them: Mum's gone, and with her the glue that held this family together; my love life's gone belly-up (as if it were ever belly-down in the first place!); Gary's set on self-destruct; Dad's about as much use as a stringless yoyo; *and* to top it all, the exams are just round the corner. For the first time ever, I can't even look at my homework. I'm just too sick at heart to even open a book.

Still, tomorrow's another day, another crummy day.

I get up and walk to the window. I twitch a corner of the curtain open and look out at the darkened streets.

Another day without you, Mum.

Next evening, after school, Adam and I bump into Gary's mate, Mick. I'd just been asking Adam if he thought Yvette was avoiding me, but Mick put a stop to that conversation.

'Heard about Adrian?' asks Mick.

'No.'

'He's got himself arrested.'

'Never!'

'Yes, it was in the paper. He robbed an office.'

'When?'

Mick rummages in his pockets. He pulls out the tiny cutting from the *Echo*. I see the date and count back. Gary was grounded when it went down. Thank God for that. He's in the clear.

'Anybody with him?'

'The usual suspects, Sean and Tony. Their parents had to go down the cop shop to pick them up. It's different with Adrian. He's seventeen. His parents don't have to be informed.'

'Where did this happen?' I ask.

'Huyton.'

'Were they in a car?'

I'm thinking blue Nissan.

'I don't know,' says Mick. 'Why?'

'Just wondering. Quick getaway, that sort of thing.'

'You've seen too many cops and robbers movies,' says Mick. 'Good job Gary wasn't with them.'

'That's for sure. Have you talked to him lately?'

'Not really. I saw him today in school. He was grumbling about being grounded.'

'Let him grumble,' I say. 'It's keeping him away from Adrian.'

He meets my eyes.

'It could be worse, you know. At least Adrian doesn't go to our school any more. Now he can't stir things up there, too.'

'He used to then?'

'Yes, he got expelled two years back. I don't think he's been in school since. Nobody will take him.'

This was Mick's idea of good news. Somehow, it doesn't lift my spirits. I think Dad needs to know.

He knows.

When I get home he is already giving Gary the third degree.

'These are the same lads you've been hanging round with, aren't they?'

'I see them sometimes,' says Gary, cool as you like.

'Sometimes?'

'You know, around.'

'So they're not close friends?'

'No, not really.'

'And this Adrian? His name keeps coming up.'

'I see him around, too.'

Gary's becoming a better liar by the day.

'Well,' says Dad, 'when you're un-grounded, I don't want you to have anything to do with them. You're starting your GCSE work next term.'

Dad notices me listening.

'Have you heard about this robbery?'

'Yes, I bumped into Mick.'

'I've just heard myself,' says Dad. 'Mick's dad collared me in the street. Haven't seen him in ages. I'm glad he came over, though. He set me straight about a few things.'

'Such as?' Gary asks.

'Such as some of the parents round here have warned

their kids to steer clear of you, you've got yourself a bad name.'

'That's rubbish!'

'So why are they saying it?'

Gary shrugs casually. That sets Dad off again.

'Are you taking this seriously?'

'Yes,' says Gary. 'I've done nothing wrong.'

I catch Gary's eye. He isn't the least bit fazed. He knows I'll keep shtum about his roll of notes. The one thing you don't do is grass.

'You know what, Gary?' Dad says. 'I don't like your attitude. I think this has gone far enough. Bottom line is, I don't want you anywhere near this Adrian. Got that?'

'Got it,' says Gary.

I'm not convinced he means it. Same goes for Dad.

Dad pops in the wash-house about nine to sort the laundry. Gary flies straight to the phone. He's making arrangements for Saturday night. He breaks off in mid-sentence when Dad comes back carrying a laundry basket full of whites.

'Have you both got clean school shirts for tomorrow?' he asks.

We nod.

'Thank goodness for that,' says Dad. 'I'm in no mood for ironing.'

I challenge Gary while Dad's making a coffee.

'Who's that you were phoning?'

Cue the usual deadpan answer.

'A mate.'

'What mate?'

'What's it to you, Sherlock?'

'If it's Adrian I'm going straight to Dad.'

Gary laughs in my face.

'You're going the right way to get caught,' I tell him.

'I won't get caught.'

'Adrian did. So did Sean and Tony. What makes you so different?'

'Look, John, I know what I'm doing.'

Yeah, and I'm going steady with Jennifer Lopez.

9

There is tension in the house. Tomorrow is the last day Gary is grounded. Saturday, he is free again. Though Dad doesn't know half the stuff I do, I know he's as nervous at the prospect as I am. He just can't see any way out. It's not like he can ground Gary forever. Around half past eight Gary wanders into the living room.

'Why don't you sit down?' says Dad. 'Watch a bit of telly with us.'

Gary snubs him.

'What for? I've got a TV in my room.'

'What I mean is, why can't we be a family for once?'

Gary lowers his head.

'We're not though, are we?'

'Meaning?'

'We don't do anything together, do we?'

I'm suddenly aware of the framed photgraphs in the corner unit. Mum, Dad and the boys at Blackpool. Mum, Dad and the boys in Talacre. Mum, Dad and the boys in Spain. There are no photos of just Dad and the boys. Nothing of us at all since she left. A big emptiness, that's all.

'John's the only one who *lives* here,' says Gary.

Dad and I exchange puzzled looks. What the heck is he on about?

'Well,' says Gary, pursuing the point. 'He is. He's always in the house with his nose in a book. It's different with us, Dad. You're always at work and me, all I do is sleep here.'

'So that's what this place means to you, is it?' says Dad, his blood pressure rising. 'A glorified doss house.'

'What's to come home for? We don't even talk. Not like I did with Mum.'

Dad's not letting him get away with that.

'What are we doing now?'

'Having a row.'

'No,' says Dad, lowering his voice, 'we're not.'

I'm expecting him to start deep-breathing exercises.

'Look, the only reason I'm always out is money. Without your mum's wages it's a struggle making ends meet. I'm only doing it for you.'

Gary nods. He can't really argue with that. One thing you can say about Dad, he's a hard worker.

'There's got to be more to life though, hasn't there?'

Dad hunches forward. It's like he's been carrying round a great weight for the last eleven months. Suddenly it has become too much to bear. He snatches at a passing straw.

'Tell you what. Let's go fishing.'

'When?'

Dad's eyes are bright. He thinks he's onto a winner.

'Tomorrow. We'll take the bivvy and stay overnight.'

Gary wishes he'd never opened his mouth but it's too late to back out.

'Well?'

'OK,' says Gary. 'You're on.'

I'm about to plead pressure of work when I notice they are actually smiling at each other. That hasn't happened in a while.

'Make that three,' I say.

Friday comes and goes. Mostly, it goes. Olivia has been doing her Me and My Microbe bit, making out she hasn't seen me. She wrinkles her nose when I'm about. I've taken to using two sorts of deodorant. I've almost bleached my

95

armpits with the stuff. As for Yvette, she seems more disappointed in me than disgusted. If anything, that's worse. I'm being boycotted by womankind whichever way you look at it.

It's good to pile into the car that night and bomb through the Mersey tunnel. For twenty four hours I'm leaving my troubles behind.

'Hand me that tent peg,' Dad is saying forty minutes later.

I'm too busy watching the clouds of flies swarming across the surface of the mere so Gary does it. I turn to look at them putting up the tent. This is something they've always had in common, the outdoor stuff. I've only ever come along for the ride.

Soon we're all set up: blankets, fishing umbrella, rods with bite alarms, fisherman's scale (you never know!), landing net.

'Anybody want anything from the shop?' Gary asks.

The shop is part of the fishery. It's mostly for hooks, line and bait but it also sells pies, sweets and drinks.

'Not for me,' says Dad.

'Hang on, Gaz,' I say. 'I'll come with you.'

Let's face it, visiting the shop is the highlight of my stay.

'That was a turn up for the book,' says Gary.

'I know what you mean. You should moan more often.'

'As opposed to knocking round with Adrian, you mean?'

He's not daft, our Gary. I think even he knows that what he's doing is wrong. But the bad lads attract him like a flame attracts moths. There's a buzz. For the first time since Mum went he feels alive. That's enough for him to suspend any thoughts of right and wrong.

I wake up in the middle of the night. We caught a couple of roach earlier, the laser bite alarm yanking us out of our sleeping bags to land the catch. It isn't the alarm this time. Somebody is moving around. I step over Dad's sleeping form and look out of the tent. There is something very still and ancient about the dead of night, like we've taken a step into eternity.

'Gary, what are you doing?'

'Here,' he whispers. 'Look at this.'

Green eyes flash in the night.

'What's that?'

'Fox. There's its mate. See?'

I do. My eyes are becoming accustomed to the moonlit darkness. The foxes are standing a few yards to our left, examining us as if we are rival predators. A slight mist clings to the mere, like a lace curtain draped over a grey disc.

'Beautiful, aren't they?'

'Yes.'

I glance at Gary.

'You'd live like this, wouldn't you?'

Gary used to go on and on to Mum about the country-side and how he would pitch a tent in the wilds and live on his wits. I prefer my creature comforts. If God wanted us to be survivalists then why did he invent the supermarket, the fridge, central heating and electric blankets? That was Mum's favourite, the electric blanket. Dad would be in the dog house for a week if he forgot to switch it on.

'Joking, aren't you?' says Gary. 'It's OK for a night but I'd rather be with my mates.'

I remember the wad of ten pound notes. The spell is broken. I thought we'd turned a corner. Maybe not.

We get home late Saturday afternoon. I'm tired, sticky and looking forward to a shower. All we've brought back is a photo of a twenty-pound carp we caught at five-fifteen this morning and half a dozen horsefly bites but we're happy all the same.

Especially Dad. He thinks he's got through to Gary. I don't want to disillusion him. We haven't been in five minutes when I hear Gary talking on his mobile. Interpreting his side of the conversation, I understand that somebody's got a job for him. You can guarantee it isn't legit. Nothing's changed. Night came to Gary eleven months ago.

He belongs to it now.

10

Right, my mind's made up. I've got to say something to Dad. I mean, Jeez, what choice do I have? This family's coming apart, and who else is going to put it back together? Dad? Gary? Don't make me laugh. But *how much* do I say? If I tell Dad too much he'll know I've been keeping things from him for weeks. So what do I do? It's not like I can let this roller coaster just run and run. It's careering out of control.

My exams are round the corner, for crying out loud.

I just can't take much more.

'And the duck says: what do you think I am, some sort of weirdo?'

Adam delivers the punchline and falls about laughing at his own joke.

'Didn't you hear me, John? The duck says—'

He realises I've got other things on my mind. He drops the quacky voice.

'Haven't you been listening to a word I've said?'

'Sorry, I was miles away.'

'Olivia?'

'I wish. No, it's everything really.'

'What's the matter now?'

I tell him about Gary's phone conversation.

'Aren't you making too much of this?' Adam says. 'It could all be perfectly innocent.'

'Adam,' I say, 'this is *Gary* we're talking about.'

I cut to the chase.

'Money is involved, Adam, and robbed cars. I don't know what else. Everything Adrian touches turns to—'

'Yes,' says Adam. 'I get the message.'

Just then the Paradise Set glide by. I don't give them a second look.

'Wow!' says Adam. 'It must be bad. You didn't even turn your head for Olivia Bellman!'

I'm aware of Olivia stopping and turning. She may think I'm the most pathetic little amoeba in the primeval soup but she still expects attention. What's the point of being gorgeous if guys don't slobber over you?

'It's bad all right.'

I've spent all morning in What-to-do-about-Gary mode. Now I've got to shift to Ohmigod-the-kiss. It's Kiss, Mark II to be precise. The lads in my class have been skitting me about it all week.

Here are just a few of their dumb lines:

Now I know why they call her Jaws.

Don't let her give you any lip, John lad.

I've heard of man-eaters, but this is ridiculous.

Yvette, the man-eating midget.

Fangs for the memory.

Half-girl, half-piranha, yes, it's super-dwarf.

Romeo and Juliet, *cannibal version.*

And on and on and rotten-on they go. Don't these divvies have anything better to do?

If the girls are giving Yvette anything like the level of stick I'm getting, she'll be mortified. She's always been on the sensitive side. I remember this time at primary school. She came in wearing bunches. One of the knuckle-draggers skitted her over them and she fled the classroom in floods of tears. I see her crossing the canteen with Ros. Just as I suspected, she's let them get to her. She looks upset. I feel guilty without quite knowing why.

Adam and I arrive at Drama a couple of minutes late. There's a crowd around Brendan.

'What's up?' Adam asks Kedra.

He's very familiar all of a sudden.

'It's Yvette. She doesn't want to be Juliet any more.'

I push my way to the front.

'Is that right?' I ask.

This is my big chance to install Olivia in her place. Suddenly, the idea doesn't appeal as much as it did, and it's got nothing to do with a baboon called Paul Martindale.

'Can I have a word with her alone?' I ask Brendan.

Brendan glances at Yvette.

'Sure, why not?'

I take her to one side.

'This is because of our kiss, isn't it?'

'What do you think?'

'So you're going to let those idiots get to you, are you?'

Yvette looks at the ground.

'Look,' I say, 'they're only having a bit of fun.'

'You call this fun?' Yvette cries.

She reels off a list of what the Paradise Set have been saying. It's horrible, really vindictive, and most of it is coming from Olivia.

'You mustn't give in to it,' I tell her.

'I thought you'd be made up,' Yvette replies. 'You get to kiss Olivia, don't you?'

'I couldn't care less about Olivia!' I retort hotly.

Hang on. Brain to mouth, what did you just say?

'Could've fooled me,' says Yvette. 'You've been drooling over her for weeks.'

'I don't drool!' I protest. 'What do you think I am, a St Bernard?'

'You drool over Olivia,' Yvette says. 'I've seen you.'

'Well, not any more,' I say, staggered at the trans-formation myself. 'Yvette, I couldn't give a monkey's about her.'

'Since when?'

Good question.

'I don't know.'

Suddenly, I know the answer.

'I'll tell you since when. Since I grew up.'

Brendan looks surprised to see a smiling Yvette restored to Verona on the Mersey.

Olivia's face is a picture of competing emotions:

* fury that she isn't the new Juliet;
* frustration that her campaign of humiliation has failed;
* confusion that her Teen Queen looks seem to have lost their magic.

I can't believe I've spent all this time moping over her. OK, so she's all Sweet Sixteen Scrumptiousness but there's nothing behind that pretty face. No, it's worse than that. There is actually quite a lot behind the pretty face, and none of it is very appealing. She's got an awful lot in common with a nest of vipers. The scales have fallen from my eyes. You wally, John, you've had the hots for a horror!

'What did you say to get Yvette back?' Adam asks.

'I said I didn't give a monkey's about Olivia.'

'What, not even a little monkey? Not even a capuchin?'

I shake my head.

'Not even a small jungle mammal,' I assure him. 'Not even a bushbaby.'

'And you mean it?'

I climb up on my high horse and declare, 'I never say anything I don't mean.'

'And this is the man that said Olivia was the girl of his dreams not a week ago!'

I tumble from my high horse and pull a face.
'Did I?'
'You did.'
'Well, I've changed my mind.'
'So who's your dream girl now?'
I find myself looking at Yvette. Adam follows my eyes.
'You don't mean—?'
No, of course I don't.
Do I?

Here we go again. Me, Romeo. Yvette, the orthodontically-challenged Juliet.
' "Thus from my lips," ' I hear myself stammer, ' "by thine, my sin is purg'd." '
I can feel the warmth of Yvette's breath. Somehow, all that awkward neck-adjusting and knee-bending doesn't seem necessary any more. The clanging awkwardness of last week is gone. We kiss and kiss . . .
I can hear people giggling.
. . . and kiss . . .
'Now that,' Brendan says approvingly, 'is passion!'
I come up for air and see Olivia looking straight at me. She's jealous. I'm not imagining it, she is actually jealous! Not jealous of me and Yvette, you understand, jealous of not being centre stage.
Turning to Yvette I say the line: ' "Give me my sin again." '
And I mean it.

'You need to make your mind up,' says Adam.
'I've made it up.'
'So who's it to be?'
'Yvette. If she'll have me.'
'Not Olivia then,' says Adam.
He doesn't sound too happy.

'So what's with the long face?' I say. 'You used to be all for me and Yvette hooking up.'

Kedra walks past and smiles. Adam smiles back.

'Oh, I get it.'

Adam looks sheepish.

'You and Kedra. How long's this been going on?'

'It isn't really going on, yet. Kedra hasn't plucked up the courage to tell Olivia, who doesn't like her friends going out with nerds.'

He does a double-take.

'Not that I'm admitting to be a nerd.'

'Well, you're nerd-ish.'

'I was hoping you'd cop off with Olivia,' he says, ignoring me. 'You know, ease my path.'

'Despite the fact that Olivia is Cruella De Vil, with a makeover?'

'Sorry, mate,' says Adam.

'Forget it.'

'So it's definitely Yvette?'

'Yes, it's Yvette. Happy for me?'

He looks longingly after Kedra then smiles and says, 'Of course not.'

I get home just before *Countdown*. I was talking to Yvette at the bus stop for fifteen minutes. I honestly couldn't tell you what we talked about. The words were just music for the lips. All the way home, I've been trying to work out how I could ever have fallen for Olivia in the first place. Was it the emptiness after Mum? Was I reacting the same way Dad did with his typist – snatching after a dream? What's for certain – it never was for real. She was like a pin-up, that's all, St Thomas's answer to Britney Spears. The trouble is, I was stupid enough to try to take her down from the wall. I walk straight into the kitchen and set the alarm off.

'That's funny,' I say out loud. 'Gary ought to be home by now.'

I switch off the alarm and reset it.

'Gary?' I call.

I don't know why. I already know he's not in.

I look round for some sign that he has been and gone. Nothing. His blazer isn't draped over the banister. His school bag isn't blocking the hallway. There you go, Poirot, proof he hasn't been home. I fall through the cloud I've been walking on since I kissed Yvette and hit the earth with a bump. I search my memory banks for a possible explanation. Homework club? Do me a favour. Detention? Maybe, but it's getting late for that. Accident? There would be something on the answering machine. I check. There are no messages. I kind of knew there wouldn't be. So I stand there alone, my insides kicked out. Gary's absence is just one more sign that we're going to Hell in a hand cart. What did you have to leave us for, Mum? We don't seem to be able to get by without you.

There is only one explanation for the empty house. Gary's out with Adrian. The job, whatever it is. The roller coaster is picking up speed.

11

OK Gary, so where are you?

First, he fails to come in from school. Then, he misses his tea. It's eleven o'clock now and well past curfew. Dad's climbing the walls. He's phoned round Gary's mates. None of them can help. Mick hasn't seen him. Same with Tony Connolly. It seems Tony's been grounded for the duration to keep him out of mischief.

'Thanks, Mr Connolly,' says Dad, hanging up. 'And you're right.'

'Right about what?' I ask.

'Adrian. The lad is poison. Trouble follows him round like a shadow.'

Dad pulls his coat off the peg.

'What are you doing?' I ask.

'I'm going for a drive round. I can't just sit here.'

I want to tell him about the blue Nissan but it seems a bit late. The damage has probably been done. Plus, he will feel betrayed if I tell him how much I've been hiding. What I'd give for a time machine.

'I've got my mobile in case he turns up,' says Dad.

He's only been out five minutes when the phone rings.

'Hello?' says a gruff voice. 'Mr Cain?'

'No, this is his son. Dad's popped out for a moment.'

'Could you get a message to him?' says the voice.

It turns out to be the police. My heart drops like a stone.

'There's no need to worry,' the officer reassures me. 'We have Gary in the custody suite.'

No need to worry! There's every need to worry.

'So you'll tell your dad to contact us?'

He leaves the extension number. I hang up and call Dad.

'Yes?'

'Dad, promise you won't flip. I know where Gary is.'

'Stupid little beggar!' Dad snarls, flooring the accelerator as he guns down the dual carriageway. 'I'll kill him.'

He doesn't actually say 'beggar'. He's too angry for that.

'Dad,' I say. 'Calm down. You don't want to get arrested for speeding.'

He takes his foot off the gas.

'You're right,' he says. 'One Cain in the cells is enough.'

I watch the retail park flashing past on the left.

'I don't believe this,' he says. 'My boy in the nick. What the Hell have I done to deserve this?'

You want me to answer that, Dad. It isn't what you've done. It's what you've failed to do.

'I'm sick of it,' he says, a groan in his voice.

There's a pub next to Copy Lane police station. We park the car there and walk round to the front entrance. I glance at the sign: Merseyside Police. This has been a long time coming.

Dad presses the buzzer for attention and a WPC comes to the door.

'It's my son,' says Dad, red as a beetroot. 'He's in the custody suite.'

The WPC smiles, and says, 'Dad doesn't look too pleased.'

That's an understatement. He looks like a crocodile who went into hospital to have a wart removed and came out as a handbag. A second officer takes us to the custody suite. We sit on grey plastic chairs and wait. And wait. And wait.

Dad jumps up and starts pacing. The sergeant glances at us from his computer then carries on working.

'Dad,' I say.

'Yes?'

I point to a whiteboard.

Written up in black dry-wipe pen are the letters: SUS UTMV THEFT.

'What does that mean?'

'Unauthorised taking of a motor vehicle. They told me over the phone.'

Gary, Sean and Adrian's names are also written on the board. Sean and Adrian have also got a second charge marked up next to their names.

'Looks like they've made quite a night of it,' says Dad.

When Gary appears he can't look us in the eye. He is chewing compulsively at a piece of skin on his thumb. Dad glares his disapproval and Gary stops.

'Would you like to talk to your son in private?' asks the officer who showed us in.

'Damned right I would!'

The officer gives a half-smile then shows the three of us into a small, shabby, side room. Gary sits down and starts chewing again. I take in the surroundings at a glance: fire regulations, alarm button, drugs initiative poster (I see Dad staring intently at that one!), formica table, three grey chairs, grey carpet (they certainly like grey in here!). There is a 'No Smoking' sign, a poster about self-harming, an awareness statement and lastly a red telephone accompanied by the notice: 'Lift Handset for Attention'.

'OK,' says Dad. 'Let's hear it.'

'We were hanging round,' says Gary.

'Where?'

'Just around.'

'No. Where? Street name. Exact details.'

'By the railway bridge.'

'Which one?'

Gary explains.

'We were sitting on the steps talking. Then Adrian turns up in his car and asks if we want to go for a drive.'

'Go on.'

'He drove us somewhere—'

Dad interrupts.

'Where?'

'I don't know. I didn't recognise it.'

He meets Dad's eyes for the first time.

'Honestly, I don't know where.'

'Fair enough,' says Dad. 'I'm sure the police will tell me. Keep talking.'

Gary's at the thumb again. Dad slaps it out of his mouth. He looks like he wants to sock Gary in the jaw. Me, I just feel numb. My flesh is creeping. What if somebody recognises me in here? What if this gets back to school somehow, to the Tomlinsons? How did this happen? I do everything right and I still end up in this crap-o-rama.

You've got no right to put us through this, Gary, no right at all.

'What happened next?' Dad snarls. 'And no lies.'

What he can't do with his fists he does with words.

'We just drove around,' Gary replies. 'Adrian stopped and got out a couple of times, then we pulled up in a car park. Adrian started burning rubber.'

Dad snorts at the phrase. Gary falters then continues.

'That's when I realised the car was stolen.'

I turn and stare at him. He looks away. I don't think Dad has noticed. I hope not.

'So you really didn't know till then?'

'I said so, didn't I!'

'Don't get lippy with me, lad! You've brought disgrace on this family so just shut it.'

Gary is finishing his story when the police officer reappears.

'Mr Cain,' he says, 'the duty solicitor is on his way.'

It is nearly an hour before the solicitor shows. I glance at my watch. How am I supposed to get up in the morning after this?

'I know,' says Dad. 'It's getting late.'

It's the first thing he has said for twenty minutes. He got everything off his chest to Gary. Since then, we have sat in silence. The only sound is the buzzing of the faulty strip light. The solicitor introduces himself.

'Rob Andrews,' he says.

He runs through what the police have told him. He mentions an off-licence.

'Off-licence? What off-licence?'

Gary stares down at his trainers. This is something he has conveniently forgotten to mention.

'It appears, Mr Cain,' says Mr Andrews, 'that the car stopped outside the Victoria Off-Licence in Park Road.'

He consults his notepad.

'Two youths – we know from the descriptions that Gary wasn't one of them—'

'Wasn't?' Dad asks as if he can't believe his luck.

'Wasn't,' Mr Andrews confirms. 'The two youths entered the off-licence and ran out with a case of Budweiser.'

'A case?' asks Dad. 'How big a case?'

The solicitor indicates with his hands. Dad confronts Gary.

'So why didn't you mention this case of booze?'

'I didn't see it.'

'Don't give me that. How do you miss something that size?'

'Honest, Dad. I didn't see them bring it in the car. I went down the alley to take a pee. Maybe that's when they did it.'

'But they were drinking?' asks Mr Andrews.

'Dunno.'

What's left of Dad's patience snaps. He starts out of his chair.

'Two cans of Budweiser were found in the front of the car,' says Mr Andrews.

'I was sitting in the back,' says Gary. 'Adrian was driving and Sean was in the passenger seat.'

They talk round and round the issue of the Budweiser then go to the arrest.

'It appears,' says Mr Andrews, 'that an off-duty police-woman saw the boys leaving the off-licence and drive off in a blue Nissan. She alerted the station. It seems the car was stolen a month ago in Southport.'

'A month ago!' Dad exclaims. 'Did you know about this, Gary?'

Gary shakes his head. For a few minutes Mr Andrews quizzes him about the ignition.

'Was the barrel broken, Gary?'

'I don't know.'

'How did Adrian turn the ignition?'

'I don't know.'

'You don't know much, do you?' says Dad.

The solicitor reads over his notes.

'So what happens now?' Dad asks.

He looks defeated, a broken man.

'The police,' Mr Andrews says, 'are satisfied that Gary was not involved in the theft of the alcohol. He was, however, being carried on a motor vehicle, knowing or believing it to be stolen.'

'*On* a motor vehicle'! Funny way of putting it. That sort of language must come straight off a charge sheet.

'I didn't know!' Gary protests.

The solicitor presses him again. It's obvious his denial won't hold up in an interview.

'Is he going to get a conviction for this?' asks Dad.

'No,' says Mr Andrews. 'I'm pretty sure he'll get away with a formal caution.'

He explains the caution. Dad sighs.

'Looks like we'll have to settle for that,' he says.

'OK,' says Mr Andrews. 'I'll have a quick word with the sergeant and be right back to you. The police will want to interview Gary and administer the caution.'

Dad nods and buries his face in his hands.

It is half past one in the morning when the police are finally done with Gary. I've had to wait outside the interview room for twenty minutes in the drizzle. There's this shaven-headed guy who's been trying to strike up a conversation with me. He's rotten drunk. I'm relieved when Dad and Gary appear. Gary takes his belongings. Dad spots a pack of cigarettes and a lighter. He hands them to the sergeant.

'Bin these for me,' he says.

The sergeant smiles. 'You want me to get rid of them?'

'Too right.'

Mr Andrews gives us his card and says goodbye. Two minutes later we are standing out in the cold, drizzly, small hours.

'Could have been worse,' says Gary.

He sounds almost chirpy. Dad grabs him by the arm and slams him against the wall, knocking the wind clean out of him.

'Could it?' he roars. 'So how's that?'

He balls his fist.

'Dad!' I cry.

He looks at me for a moment then unclenches the fist and lets Gary go.

'I could kill you, Gary,' he says, desperation crackling

through his voice. 'Think you're big, do you? Think you're clever?'

Gary's face twists.

'No.'

'No,' says Dad. 'You're not big and you're not clever. You're just a pathetic, little scally. You're wrecking our lives.'

With that, Dad heads for the car. Gary and I exchange glances. Before we get in, Dad has one more thing to say.

'Listen to me, both of you,' he says, low and almost menacing. 'This doesn't go beyond the three of us. You don't tell your friends, you don't tell my mum and dad, and most of all you don't tell Gran and Grandad Ferguson. We don't wash our dirty linen in public, not even in front of family. Got that?'

'Got it.'

None of us speaks on the way home. The moment we walk through the door, Dad jerks a thumb in the direction of Gary's room.

'Get up there, you. I don't even want to talk to you.'

Dad glances at the clock. It's ten past two.

'Look at the time! I'm up again at five. Then there's you, John. This won't have done your revising much good.'

'I'll be OK.'

'OK!' says Dad. 'I don't know if anything will ever be OK again.'

12

I don't like Tuesdays. Especially this Tuesday. How am I supposed to keep this Gary thing to myself? I usually tell Adam everything. But not this time. I promised Dad.

'Something wrong?' Adam asks.

'No,' I say. 'Not really.'

'It's Gary then?'

He's not daft, Adam.

'Well, that's still going on.'

I can't say any more.

'Has something happened?' Adam asks.

I shake my head and look away. I hate lying to my best friend. What's more, I really hate Tuesdays. No PE, no free periods, no Drama, nothing to break up the diet of revision.

'I've asked Kedra out,' says Adam.

Oh joy! A diversion.

'What did she say?'

'We're going to the cinema on Friday night.'

'Never!'

Adam grins.

'It's true.'

'So do the other members of the Paradise Set know?'

Adam shrugs.

'I don't know and I don't care. She's too good for them.'

'It's only yesterday you were trying to set me up with Olivia,' I remind him.

'Sorry about that,' says Adam. 'Pure selfishness. I was

right first time round. You and Yvette, you were made for each other.'

'What, in spite of the height difference?'

'Of course. You can always get her a pair of stilts. Alternatively, saw your legs off at the knee.'

'Full of helpful suggestions, aren't you?'

Adam smiles.

'Overflowing, John lad. Hey, why not ask Yvette if she wants to come along Friday night? We could make it a foursome.'

'Are you sure that's such a good idea?'

'Why not?'

'I don't even know if she'll go out with me yet.'

'There's only one way to find out.'

Adam points. A small, freckle-faced girl is heading our way. Her smile is as big as she is. It's Yvette.

'That kiss,' I say the moment we're alone. 'It was good, wasn't it? You weren't disappointed?'

'No, John, I wasn't disappointed.'

The way she says it! Throaty, encouraging. A warm sensation spreads from my knees up through my stomach to my chest and throat. What with everything that's happened at home, I'd almost forgotten what this feels like. I think it's called happiness. My face starts to burn.

'I was thinking,' I say haltingly. 'Maybe we could—you know—go out sometime.'

'When?'

The word leaves her lips like a rifle shot. Maybe Yvette thinks that sounds a bit too eager because she immediately adds, 'When—roughly?'

It's my turn to smile. How could I ever have been so stupid? She likes me. She's always liked me. For over a year it's been pretty obvious that she doesn't just like me as a friend. Just how pretty, decent and likeable she is has just kind of crept up on me while I was staring at the Bimbo Queen. Forget the braces and the lack of stature. While I was looking the other way all that time, she became more than pretty: she's beautiful. I look down at the morning sunlight on her hamster cheeks and her freckles and I want to kiss her.

She says, 'Later.'

'I'll hold you to that.'

I'm jogging over to Adam when I remember I was meant to be fixing up the date. I jog back over to her.

'What about Friday?' I ask.

'Friday's good.'

'A movie?'

'Great,' she says. 'We'll talk it over later.'

'Right, see you in the canteen.'

By 3.30 p.m. I don't hate Tuesdays at all. Even double Science hasn't pulled me down off Cloud Nine. I see Yvette to her bus. We kiss while we're waiting. I notice Olivia getting into the front passenger seat of her dad's car. He'll be ferrying her to tennis coaching or extra tuition or some such thing. She's what you could call a driven girl. She's staring at us. For her benefit I kiss Yvette even more passionately.

'Hey,' says Yvette. 'Let a girl come up for air.'

'Can't blame me for being keen.'

'Of course not,' Yvette answers with a heart-stopping smile. 'But you wouldn't want us getting tangled up again, would you?'

I hold her tight until her bus arrives.

The phone rings just before eleven.

'Who's that?' Dad grumbles.

He was half-asleep in his chair.

'I'll get it,' I tell him.

It's Tony Connolly's dad. He sounds worried.

'You haven't seen anything of our Tony, have you?' he says. 'Only he's gone AWOL. I haven't seen him since last night.'

'I'll get Gary.'

I'm no more than an arm's length all the while Gary is talking. He's non-commital, evasive even. All he will say is he hasn't been out and he hasn't seen Tony. Dad arrives and reaches for the phone.

'Can I have a word?' he says.

Gary hands over the phone.

'Mr Connolly? It's Phil Cain. What's happened?'

He listens and fixes Gary with a suspicious glare.

'No, nothing to do with Gary this time. He's grounded. I know. They're a worry, all right. Sorry I can't help.'

He hangs up.

'Do you know anything, Gary?'

Gary puts on his victim grimace.

'How could I? I haven't been out.'

'And you haven't spoken to Tony?'

'I told you, my phone charger's broken.'

Dad points to the house phone.

'There's always this one.'

'I don't talk to my mates on this line,' says Gary. 'Not since you said you were going to check the itemised bill.'

Dad isn't happy but he lets it go.

'Just don't give me any more grief, Gary. I couldn't stand it.'

Gary turns his back and climbs the stairs.

'Don't worry,' he says.

I wake up and smile the moment the sleep-haze has cleared from my head. My good mood doesn't last long.

I'm unlocking the back door when Gary comes rushing up.

'Where are you going?'

'The wash-house.'

'What do you want from there?'

'My trainers.'

'You have your breakfast,' Gary says. 'I'll get them.'

Did Gary just offer to do something for me? That's spooky. Even spookier is the loud bang from the wash-house.

'What's that?'

'I didn't hear anything.'

Dad went to work an hour ago so it isn't him. Now, I don't believe in poltergeists and, as far as I know, the local mice haven't started wearing concrete-soled boots. I push past Gary and shove open the wash-house door. I meet resistance.

'OK,' I say. 'Who's in here?'

Tony comes to the door, followed by Sean.

'Gary, you idiot,' I say, 'Dad will kill you.'

'Then don't tell him.'

'Tell these idiots to clear off and I just might consider it.'

'John—'

I flip open my mobile.

'Tell them.'

'You heard,' says Gary. 'You'd better go. See you.'

'Tony,' I say. 'Call your dad. He's worried sick.'

Tony gives me a look made of barbed wire.

'What's it to you?'

The moment they're gone I get my trainers from the wash-house and look round. It's obvious from the state of the place that they've slept the night here.

'Get it tidied,' I tell Gary. 'What are you doing, turning it into a doss house?'

Hear that? I really am turning into Dad. I shove my face right into Gary's. He doesn't so much as blink.

'I'm getting my bus in ten minutes,' I tell him. 'Don't let them back in the house when I'm gone.'

'I won't.'

'You'd better not. I can still tell Dad.'

Irritation sparks through the air.

'I won't, OK.'

As I walk up the street I don't feel one bit reassured.

I've got my speech worked out. I know what I've got to say to Dad. On my way home from school I've been telling myself not to let Gary sweet-talk me out of it. There's fat chance of that. You would think this morning never happened. He just sits there eating his pot noodle. I hate him and he hates me. Sibling rivalry has gone nuclear. Dad walks in at half past five and drops his work bag on the table. He looks grey.

'Bad day?' I ask.

'No,' says Dad. 'Just a long one. I was in at half past four.'

'How come?'

'We had an emergency call out.'

He explains. I nod as though I know what he's talking about.

'We could do with a lock on the wash-house,' I say, out of the blue.

Gary stiffens.

'Why?'

'There was hair all over my school jumper this morning,' I tell him. 'I think next door's cat has been getting in.'

'Fair enough,' says Dad. 'We don't want the neighbourhood strays using it.'

'Too right,' I say looking pointedly at Gary.

'You'll find a padlock in that carrier bag in the spare room.'

I go and get it.

'I'll do it straight away.'

I walk past Gary and add, 'You can't be too careful.'

13

We go through the GCSE timetable, highlighting our exams and transferring them into diaries. Suddenly, a date leaps off the page.

'How could I have forgotten?'

'Did you say something?' Adam asks.

'It's OK. It's just family stuff.'

He gives me a funny look.

'Oh.'

I look out the window. It's like I'm seeing for the first time in weeks.

'Gary,' I call as I walk in the house. 'Are you in?'

'Through here.'

He's channel-surfing.

'Shift yourself, Gaz. We're cooking tea for the old man.'

'Are you serious?'

'Deadly serious.'

Gary's watching the Teletubbies. Fourteen going on four.

'You cook. I'm busy.'

I switch the set off.

'I was watching that!'

'Gary, even you've grown out of Tinky Winky. Are you going to help with the tea or not?'

'Not.'

'Odd that,' I say. 'I thought you hated being grounded.'

Well, whaddya know, I've got his attention.

'What's that supposed to mean?'

'The more you do round the house the quicker you get your freedom back.'

'Right, you've convinced me. What do I do?'

Neither of us is much of a Jamie Oliver. I can just about manage chili con carne and spaghetti bolognese. Gary can do pot noodle, baked beans and fried egg. We decide on chili.

'That's Dad,' I say, hearing his car pull up. 'Put the rice on, Gaz.'

'What's that smell?' Dad asks.

'We made the tea.'

Dad is immediately suspicious.

'Why, what have you been up to?'

'Nothing.'

The colour is dropping out of his face.

'It's Gary again, isn't it?'

'Gary's here. He's boiling the rice.'

Dad's mind is doing overtime. It's fun watching the confusion.

'So what's the occasion?'

'Nothing.'

The occasion can wait till later.

I'm about to mention the very important date when the phone rings.

'You answer it, Dad,' I say. 'Gary and I will wash up.'

'We will?'

'Brownie points,' I remind him. 'Lots and lots of Brownie points.'

I'm rinsing the colander when Dad exclaims, 'Are you serious?'

Gary and I exchange glances.

'No, no, I understand,' says Dad, his voice suddenly warm.

A woman?

'Tomorrow night?' he says. 'Yes, that would be great.'

Definitely a woman.

'Thanks so much for calling.'

A very important woman.

Gary puts away the last of the dishes and returns to the TV.

'Who was that on the phone?' I ask.

'Rose.'

Dad looks stunned.

'What, the one who grabbed you in the fruit bats?'

'The same.'

'So, what did she want?'

'A second date.'

'And you said yes?'

'Yes, it seems I mis-read the signals. She was reaching for my hand and got lost in the dark. She was as embarrassed as I was. It's taken her this long to pluck up the courage to call me.'

'You like her then?'

He nods.

I postpone mentioning the very important date. The timing wouldn't be right.

A couple of hours later, Gary's making a fuss.

'I'm fourteen,' he pouts. 'I don't need a babysitter.'

'Well, tough,' says Dad. 'I've already asked Gran to come round.'

'Dad, this is humiliating.'

Dad hesitates.

'You promise you'll stay in? No sneaking out just because John and I aren't here?'

Gary does his ET impression.

'I'll be right here.'

'Fair enough, but I'll be phoning you to check.'

'Dad, I said I'd be in, didn't I?'

'Go on, then,' says Dad. 'But no mates and no meeting Adrian. He's strictly *persona non grata*.'

Gary promises to behave. He sounds genuine.

So how come I feel this prickle down the back of my neck?

Yvette's face lights up the moment she sees me. It dims when she sees Adam and Kedra.

'I didn't know there would be anyone else,' she says.

Her eyes say: especially not *her*. I wonder if I'm completely insensitive. I should have realised this might be embarrassing. I'm asking Yvette to spend the evening with one of Olivia's best friends, one of the girls who's been making her life a misery.

'Sorry, I didn't think—'

'That's the trouble,' says Yvette. 'You never do.'

She turns to go.

'Yvette, don't.'

Kedra comes over.

'This is because of me, isn't it? Look Yvette, I know I've been horrible to you. Olivia winds us up to do it. She's quite a nice person really. She just—'

'What?'

Yvette's eyes are brimming with tears but she refuses to play the victim.

'She does have a cruel streak,' Kedra admits.

'So you all have to join in like a flock of sheep?'

Kedra looks down.

'Sorry.'

'Why don't we split up,' says Adam. 'We can always meet up again later.'

'Is that all right?' I ask.

Yvette dabs at her eyes with a tissue.

'Sure.'

I'm still apologising on the way home. I tell you, I could grovel for England.

'John, I'm not angry.'

I'm not sure I believe her. After the year I've had, this thing with Yvette is too good to be true.

'Sure?'

Her hand slips into mine.

'Positive.'

Our bus goes straight to Yvette's. If I see her home I've got a twenty-minute walk back to my place, but who cares? I want to be with her as long as I can. We sit holding hands and talk about the stuff we got up to when we were little. Neither of us can believe the way things have turned out. I walk her to her door and kiss her goodnight, just like in the old movies.

'I'll see you on Monday.'

'We could do something this weekend.'

'We could?'

'I'll phone you.'

The quickest way home means going up County Road. I'm heading in that direction when I glimpse movement in the corner of my eye. This isn't one of my favourite places late at night. You get a lot of gangs. Adam got head-butted once round here coming back from his nan's. I glance up at the shop roofs. I'm sure I saw something.

A man out walking his dog says, 'They're always up there.'

'I beg your pardon?'

'Kids, up on the roof.'

I carry on looking. There's somebody up there all right.

'I wish I had one of those mobile phones,' the man says. 'I'd call the coppers.'

He walks away.

'Hooligans.'

When he's gone, I look up again. The figure I see is Sean. I walk round the back. There are three, no four, other lads. Oh, Gary, you wouldn't. Not on this night of nights. Not when I'm finally starting to feel good about myself. Across the road the Paradise Bingo is letting out.

'Look at them,' says one woman.

Her friend has a mobile. She starts punching in a number.

'Police?' she says.

I've got to act and act now.

'Gary!' I yell.

The figures on the roof stiffen. Then I see them running. Alerted by my shout the women look at me.

'That's one of them,' they say. 'He's their look-out.'

I'm too far away to be recognised but I'm not hanging round. I race back to County Road. I'm almost at the flyover before I dare walk normally again. I hear a police siren, then another. Seconds later a vehicle roars past me. It's blue, but a Fiesta this time. Adrian likes blue. I'm jogging past Sainsbury's when a third police car passes us. I hear the *whacka-whacka-whacka* of the police helicopter overhead. A searchlight rakes the city below.

'I'll kill you, Gaz.'

As I turn into our road, Dad is getting out of the car. I follow him through the door.

He's shouting to Gary.

'Everything OK?' he asks.

I wait. What if there's no reply? As it turns out, Gary's in.

'Sure, why wouldn't it be?'

Dad winks at me and goes in the kitchen.

'I called a couple of times,' he says, keen to claim the title Superdad. 'The second time was about nine o'clock. He said he was bored and he was going to bed. I left it after that. You can't be on at him all the time, can you?'

Going to bed? Oh, very clever, Gary. So that's how you did it.

'How was your date?' Dad asks.

'Great.'

I still don't feel too comfortable about this woman of Dad's but why act miserable? I force out the reply.

'Yours?'

He smiles.

'I had a really good time. She's lovely.'

Lovely isn't a word I wanted to hear. Talking this way feels like I'm betraying Mum, but I manage a joke anyway.

'No grabbing you in the fruit bats?'

'No, nothing like that. Anyway, do you mind locking up?'

'I've got a few things to do first,' I tell him. 'I'll do it in a minute.'

'No hurry. Goodnight, son.'

I wait for Dad's door to shut, then sneak up to Gary's door.

'Gary? Gaz?' I whisper.

'What?'

'Was that you tonight?'

'I don't know what you're on about.'

'I saw Sean. He was on the roof of the supermarket in County Road.'

'Didn't Dad tell you?' Gary asks. 'I was in all night. He phoned to check.'

'Yes, but Dad didn't phone again after nine.'

'I was in bed.'

Suddenly, I'm not so sure. What if Gary's telling the truth?

'So you didn't sneak out?'

'What's with the third degree?'

'I told you, I saw Sean.'

'Yes? Well, you didn't see me.'

I go back down to lock up. I'm beginning to think I've misjudged Gary when I notice his trainers by the front door. They are caked with fresh mud.

14

Next morning starts with a row. The moment Dad goes out to the shops I tackle Gary.

'You're a liar.'

'You what?'

'I saw the state of your trainers. They were caked in mud.'

'So?'

'Well, they didn't get that way staying in the house, did they?'

Gary's even got an answer for that.

'I was sorting my fishing stuff on the lawn. Dad says I can go fishing when my grounding is over.'

He tries to push past.

'Happy now?'

'No.'

Gary is halfway down the hall when he shouts back, 'Well, tough!'

Dad's really pleased with himself when he gets in with the shopping. From one of the carrier bags he pulls a single red rose in a presentation box and a card. He hands it to me.

'A rose for my Rose,' I read.

This is well tacky.

'Not too corny?'

'Much too corny,' I say. 'But she's a woman, isn't she? She'll love it to bits.'

He grins like a naughty toddler.

'So, when are you seeing her again?'

'I was thinking of taking her out for a meal tonight.'

I feel a kick in my chest.

'Tonight?'

'Why, have you got something planned?'

'No, it isn't that.'

'What then?'

How do I do this?

'I think you ought to be here, for Gary.'

I see Dad's good mood disintegrating before my very eyes.

'Why, what's happened?'

I hesitate.

'Nothing. I just think it's a good idea to be around. He's still—restless.'

'You're right,' says Dad. 'It's only two minutes since he was riding round in a robbed car. I've got to be here for him.'

Oh joy!

'Rose can come round here instead.'

Oh puke!

That evening I'm round Yvette's. We sit on the wall in front of her house, talking. Yvette's feet don't reach the pavement so she just lets them swing. A nectarine sun is glancing off the window panes. I've caught her mum a couple of times peeking at us through the net curtains. I remember something Dad said: if you want to see what your girlfriend will look like in a few years' time, look at her mother. I smile at Mrs Tomlinson. I could do worse.

'She's all right, your mum,' I tell her. 'You're lucky.'

Yvette picks up the vibe immediately.

'You must really miss your mum,' she says.

'Yes, every day.'

Every single day. Since I saw the date on the calendar I've been thinking about her even more than usual.

'How do you handle that?' Yvette says. 'One of the most important people in your life. Suddenly one day they're gone.'

'Handle it?' I say. 'You don't—You can't. People say the hurt fades. I'm still waiting.'

Yvette has moved closer. I can feel her breath on my face. She's offering to listen.

'You get by,' I tell her, trying to explain feelings I can't yet explain to myself. 'She's what made our family tick, you see. She didn't make a big song or dance about it, but things happened because of her. Everything seemed to go so smoothly. Now the house is empty without her. It's the little things. Nobody puts the ties round the curtains in the morning. The beds don't get changed so often. We don't have air fresheners any more. Or flowers.'

Yvette giggles.

'What?' I ask.

'So that's it, you're starting to smell?'

You're right, Yvette, but not the way you mean. The thing is, but for you, *life* stinks. The thought brings me down to earth.

'I shouldn't be here,' I say.

Yvette looks disappointed.

'No,' I add quickly. 'It's got nothing to do with you. You're the best thing in my life.'

Her face flushes with pleasure.

'You mean it?'

'I never say anything I don't mean.'

'You said you were mad about Olivia Bellman.'

What did she have to bring that up for?

'Yvette!'

'It's all right. I'm only teasing. So why shouldn't you be here?'

I give her a sanitised version of Gary's recent track record. I don't want to scare her off.

'He's been hanging round with some real pondlife,' I tell her by way of conclusion. I try a bit of humour.

'They're the lads your mother's warned you about.'

'Then you must do your duty,' says Yvette.

'Thanks for understanding.'

Yvette knows as well as I do that her mum's been spying on us. She gives the window a glance then pulls me close and kisses me. As I walk up the street I can still taste her on my lips.

My arrival coincides with Rose's. She's wearing a white blouse and a flowered skirt. Dad meets her at the door. I can't remember the last time he looked so happy. I still can't bring myself to think this is right, but I decide to make an effort, for Dad's sake. He tries not to let on, big boys don't cry and all that, but he does cry. I heard him once in the early hours, sobbing like a baby. I give Rose the once-over. She's tall, attractive, with bobbed, black hair. That, and the glasses, make me wonder if she isn't a librarian or something.

'Hi, Rose,' says Dad. 'Welcome to the Ponderosa.'

The what?

'This is John, my eldest.'

'Hello, John.'

'Don't you work with animals?' I ask.

I almost add: especially fruit bats.

'No,' says Rose. 'I'm a librarian. The animals are a hobby.'

There, I *knew* she was a librarian.

The introduction to Gary doesn't go quite so smoothly.

'This is my younger boy, Gary.'

'Hello, Gary,' says Rose.

Gary walks past her without a word. Dad and I exchange glances.

'Hormones,' he tells Rose by way of explanation.

Rose nods.

'I understand.'

While Dad is sweet-talking Rose in the kitchen, I tackle Gary.

'That was out of order.'

'Get off my case.'

'What's Rose done to you?'

'I said: leave it.'

'You don't need to be so rude,' I tell him, putting down my size nine right in the middle of the minefield that is Gary's emotions. 'I feel a bit funny about him bringing somebody home, but we've got to move on.'

'Really?' says Gary, rounding on me. 'You want to know why I wouldn't talk to her? Did you see what Dad gave her?'

I'm trying to get on his wavelength.

'It was a rose.'

The cogs are turning, but I haven't got there yet.

'That's Mum's flower,' Gary reminds me.

'Oh.'

He's right. Why didn't I think of that?

'All the fine words at the funeral,' says Gary. 'He's soon forgotten, hasn't he?'

'Oh, come off it, Gary. It's only because of her name: a rose for his Rose.'

Gary's head snaps round.

'Is that what he said?'

'Does it matter?'

Stupid question. It matters all right. He tries to get past me.

'Get out of my way.'

I block his way.

'Not until you calm down. You're not the only one who misses Mum.'

Then I hear my own voice. I can hardly believe what I'm saying.

'But it's nearly a year, Gaz. Is it so bad that Dad's seeing someone?'

Gary stares me down.

'If you gave a damn about Mum,' he says, 'you wouldn't even have to ask.'

I've had enough.

'Take that back,' I yell, shoving him.

In return, he lashes out with his elbow and we crash into the wardrobe, wrestling and punching. Before I know it, Dad is separating us. His eyes are bulging and a vein is throbbing in his temple.

'Well, thanks a bunch,' he says. 'I'm trying to entertain a lady and this is how you behave.'

'Lady?' Gary sneers. 'Is that what you call her?'

Dad spins round.

'What did you say?'

'A rose for your Rose, eh? You make me sick!'

Dad stares first at Gary, then at me.

'Get to your rooms, the pair of you. I'll speak to you later.'

Rose goes about ten o'clock. Dad comes storming upstairs the moment she's gone.

I'm first for the third degree.

'Well, what was all that about? I thought you knew how important this evening was to me.'

'Sorry.'

'So, what were you fighting about?'

'Talk to Gary.'

'No, I want to hear it from you.'

My eyes slip away from his.

'It's the rose.'

'What?'

'Mum's flower.'

There's a groan deep in Dad's throat.

'John, I didn't think.'

Now I've started, it's hard to stop.

'When you're a kid,' I explain, 'your mum's invincible. You expect her to be there forever. Then—'

I'm fighting to get the words out.

'Then she isn't. When she was around life was always so easy, you see, so safe.'

Finally, I look at him.

'Now everything is changing. There's this new woman on the scene. It's a bit hard to take, that's all.'

Dad's anger has completely evaporated.

'You think I don't care,' he says. 'Is that it?'

I'm not sure how to answer.

'I'm not saying that. It's just—It's different. I want life back the way it was.'

Dad nods.

'Yes, me too. It can't happen though, can it? I'm lonely, son, that's the top and bottom of it. Maybe I'm weak, I don't know, but the feeling won't go away. I'm so empty inside. I need someone. I mean, you lads are everything to me, but I need—'

I save him the trouble of trying to explain.

'Yes, Dad, I know.'

He looks in the direction of Gary's room.

'I'd better have a word with him,' he says. 'I'll go easy.'

'Before you go, Dad, there's something I need to ask you.'

I explain my idea about the date on the calendar.

'OK,' says Dad. 'I'll give it some thought. Now for Gary.'

A moment later, I hear him shout from the far end of the landing.

'John, check downstairs. He isn't here.'

I run downstairs. There is a tell-tale sign that he has done a runner: the front door is wide open.

'What time did he show up?' Adam asks the next day.

'One o'clock in the morning. Dad was going spare.'

'Did he explain himself?'

'No, he just went to bed. He said he'd been walking. After what I said to Dad, the old man decided to let it go at that.'

Adam sends a stone skipping over the pond. We've come to Croxteth Park for a change of scenery.

'Your Gary is getting himself in deep,' says Adam.

'Tell me about it. It's like living with Semtex.'

'Time to ride back?'

I look across the park.

'I wish I could pitch a tent here and forget I had a home.'

'You don't mean that.'

'Don't I?'

Both sets of grandparents are there when I get in.

'Where's Gary?' I ask.

'Out back,' Dad says. 'I'm paying him a fiver to tidy the garden.'

'We've been talking about your idea,' says Grandad Ferguson. 'We think it's a grand idea.'

'You do?'

'Yes, we're going to book a venue.'

I can hear Gary mowing the lawn.

'I'm always doing the garden,' I say. 'How come he gets paid for it?'

'We wanted him out of the way,' says Grandma Cain.

'Why?'

'That young man's had a difficult year. He's not as strong as you.'

Strong? Somebody thinks I'm strong! Well, they're not

136

in my room next to me late at night when I look into the darkness and wonder how I'll get through the next day. They're not around when I stand in the garden looking up at the sky and wonder if life will ever be as good as it was before the crash.

'We all know how badly he took Lisa's accident. We thought this masterplan of yours might be a nice surprise for him, so no giving the game away.'

'It'll come just at the right time for you, too,' says Dad. 'Straight after the exams. We can all blow off some steam.'

I look round. I just hope Gary doesn't do something stupid in the meantime.

I go out to Gary. He's raking the grass cuttings.

'Need a hand?'

'Sure, if you want. I'm not splitting the fiver though.'

'Did Dad give you much grief over last night?'

'No, not really.'

He fixes me with a cold stare.

'And don't ask me where I went.'

'I won't. Gary, you've got everybody worried.'

'Who's everybody?'

'Me, Dad, the grandparents.'

'So, you're worried, are you? How interesting. Thanks for the information.'

I drop the grass into the cuttings bin.

'We're only trying to help.'

'Sure, you're a regular bunch of Samaritans.'

'Talk to me, Gary. It doesn't have to be this way.'

Gary puts the mower in the shed and padlocks it.

'Go on then, what do you want to talk about: football, the weather, general knowledge? Maybe we could discuss the stock market. Go on, over to you, what's your starter for ten?' He kicks the grass off his trainers. 'Forget it, John. Go and play shrink with some other mug.'

'Gary, why are you being like this?'

'You really want to know?' he says. 'Because this is who I am and I don't plan to change. Not for you—' He shoves past, knocking me off balance. '—not for anybody.'

15

'Are you feeling nervous?' Yvette asks.

'Yes, a bit.'

This is it, the public performance which Mrs Owen has helpfully tacked on to the end of our GCSE course. Some of the parents have had their grumbles, especially the Bellmans, but nothing Mrs O can't handle. Even in a school like St Thomas's, there are parents who think education is more than exams. Mrs Owen introduces the show.

'As you all know,' she begins, 'our pupils begin Study Leave on Friday. I'm sure you all remember how stressful this time of year can be. I hope you will understand that this performance is meant to reduce, rather than increase the stress.'

This is received in complete silence. Peeking through the curtains I can see the Bellmans. They're looking particularly stone-faced.

'OK, people,' Mrs Owen says to us, 'I've warmed them up.'

Do I detect a touch of irony there?

'Go out and enjoy yourself.'

I swap glances with Yvette and we both start giggling. Mrs Owen taps me on the shoulder and gives me a mock glare of disapproval.

'Just don't enjoy it too much.'

There's a short wine-and-cheese do after the performance.

Make that fruit juice and cheese for the performers! The Bellmans have dragged Olivia back from her tantrum. At the moment they've got poor Brendan pinned in the corner. His deck pumps are curling with embarrassment.

'They're giving old Brendan the third degree,' says Adam.

'Pushy people, the Bellmans,' I say. 'They probably want to know whether Olivia can make it in the movies.'

'Yes,' says Yvette. 'As Godzilla.'

'Hang on a minute,' says Kedra. 'She's still a friend of mine, remember.'

'Yes,' says Adam. 'But you have to admit she can be a pain.'

Kedra gives a half-smile.

'Sometimes.'

I draw Yvette to one side.

'You're getting good at sticking up for yourself.'

'Thanks.'

Dad and Gary wander over.

'Are you ready to make a move?' says Dad.

Shakespeare isn't really his thing. He'd prefer *Die Hard* or *Terminator*. As for Gary, he deserves an Oscar for his performance as First Bored Teenager. I bet he complained and whined his way through the whole evening. I'm just glad I was up on stage where I couldn't hear him.

'I'll just say goodbye to Yvette,' I tell Dad.

'Go on then,' he says. 'She's right here.'

That's when he realises what I mean.

'Oh, right, we'll be in the car.'

'She's a nice girl, that Yvette,' says Dad.

'Yes,' Gary grunts. 'For a dwarf.'

Lucky for him he's in the front seat where I can't get at him.

'Shut it, you!'

'Touchy. I only said—'

'I know what you said. Yvette's worth a thousand of your stupid mates. So keep your mouth shut or I'll shut it for you.'

Gary has to have the last word.

'There's me going easy by not mentioning the braces.'

I make a grab for him.

'Knock it off, lads,' says Dad. 'I'm trying to drive here. There's no sense spoiling the evening.'

'How do you spoil something that stinks already?' says Gary. 'What did I have to go for anyway?'

'Drop it, Gary,' says Dad. 'Or do I have to remind you why you're grounded?'

We're coming down Moss Lane when a car flashes its lights and blares its horn.

'What's the matter with him?' Dad asks.

I turn to see the car roaring past the Bingo Hall. The tail lights flash as it corners. It's a blue Fiesta.

'Joyriders,' I say. Pointedly.

Gary doesn't say a word.

The phone is ringing when we come through the door. I answer it. It's Tony Connolly's dad again.

'Dad,' I say, 'it's Mr Connolly.'

Gary's expression doesn't change.

'Hello?' says Dad. 'Oh, not again. Sorry, I haven't seen Tony. No, our Gary is still grounded. It's bound to be this Adrian character.'

Mr Connolly tells Dad something.

'So that's all he's getting, community service? They ought to lock him up and throw away the key.'

Dad isn't usually the Law and Order type but in Adrian's case he'd go for the electric chair.

'He's a real a piece of work. Fancy getting your kicks out of leading younger lads astray.'

Gary snorts his disagreement and walks away.

'Now, don't go doing something you'd regret,' Dad tells Mr Connolly. 'I know how you feel but if you hit him you're the one who gets in trouble.'

'What was all that about?' I ask when Dad hangs up.

'Mr Connolly's on the warpath. He's after Adrian's address. I think he's going to do him some damage.'

'You wouldn't take the law into your own hands, would you?'

'No,' says Dad, 'but only because I might get caught.'

Three days later Adam has some news for me.

'Did you hear about Adrian?' he asks.

'No.'

'Mum heard Sean talking at school. Tony Connolly's dad got hold of him. He broke his nose and knocked out a couple of teeth.'

'Is Mr Connolly in trouble?'

'I don't think so. The police weren't called. It won't stop Adrian, though.'

'It would stop me,' I say.

'You're not like Adrian. You haven't been excluded from two schools.'

'Yes,' I say. 'I know, well, about one of his exclusions anyway.'

'Really? Well, maybe you don't know everything. It seems he's been done over before, and he still came back for more. It goes with the territory. He's always fighting. Wins some, loses some. He likes the attention. It adds to the hard man image. The broken nose will just make him look tough. What I'm telling you, John, is this isn't going to go away.'

'And you think Mr Connolly's done more harm than good?'

'Definitely,' Adam says. 'Now Tony hates his old man more than ever.'

We could be talking about Gary.

Saturday afternoon I'm walking down Church Street hand in hand with Yvette. Adam and Kedra are walking behind. It's our last walk in the sun before the exams.

'Any idea how to find Littlewood's?' Kedra asks with a twinkle in her eye.

'Ouch,' I say. 'Low blow.'

Yvette wants to know what we're talking about. Adam explains. Yvette goes moody for a moment or two. I decide to leave well alone. We're sitting in St John's Gardens when she pops the question.

'What did you ever see in Olivia?'

'Looks,' I answer. 'That's all.'

So what am I, Yvette is probably asking, the back of a bus?

'You know what it's like. She's tall, blonde. She turns heads. It's what lads go for.'

Correct me if you will, but didn't I just commit suicide? I even mentioned that Olivia is tall! How sensitive is that when you're talking to a girl who doesn't have to bend to limbo dance? Then a flash of inspiration comes.

Got it!

'She was an image, you see, not a real girl. Sometimes you fall in love with the idea of being in love. It's something you do.'

'I didn't,' Yvette says simply.

'Didn't what?'

'Go for the conventional. You know what I mean, the Paul Martindale type.'

She *is* toughening up! That's it, knock my self-esteem too.

'Listen, Yvette, I'm no good at this. It was a stupid crush. I always thought of you as a mate until—'

'Yes?'

143

'Until this.'

I kiss her. Now stop asking stupid questions!

'Hey, knock it off, you two,' says Adam. 'Anyone for a walk to the Albert Dock?'

So we set off hand in hand. That's Yvette and me holding hands, you understand, not Adam and me. You could take this buddy stuff too far!

'Did you have a nice time?' Dad asks.

I close the front door behind me.

'Yes, it's just a pity the exams have to spoil it.'

'You'll be glad you put the work in when you get a good job,' says Dad.

Very original!

I see Gary sitting on the garden path.

'What's he doing?'

'He's getting his fishing gear ready. We're going out to the mere again. Have you forgotten?'

'No, I remembered.'

'We're leaving about six.'

There's something different this time. There's no magic. We hardly exchange a word. Going fishing is like putting sticking plaster on a broken leg. We're way past boys' days out. When it comes to male bonding we're all out of glue. Through the tent flap I can see Gary crouched over his rod. He looks so alone. Later, just like the last time, I wake up in the small hours.

'Gary?'

There's no answer.

'Gaz?'

I slide out of my sleeping bag, pull on my trackie bottoms and slip into my trainers.

This time there is no fox. It's more like a wolf.

'Gary?'

He's standing in a clump of trees talking on his mobile, the one he says he can't charge. I try to overhear what he's saying but he's too far away.

You idiot, Gary.

16

We've just reached halfway in our exams. It was French today. That's another difference between Gary and me: I like languages; I love the challenge of actually trying to sound French or German. As for Gary, he doesn't even seem to like his own language. Let's face it, he doesn't even speak it that well! He interrupts me talking to myself in French. He thinks anybody who likes books and learning is a complete divvy.

'Why do they have to talk funny?' he sneers. 'Why can't they just speak English?'

'That's just it,' I retort. 'They do, and better than us. Better than you anyway.'

I try to explain that you can find loads of people abroad who can speak English, but precious few Brits who can manage more than a couple of words in anyone else's language.

'That's my point,' says Gary. 'If they can speak English, why should we speak Frog?'

'Just listen to yourself, will you!' I cry. 'What makes you think you're better than everybody else?'

Dad walks in on us.

'What's up now?'

'He's a philistine,' I say.

'Yes? Well, you're a div,' says Gary.

'You don't even know what a philistine is,' I retort. 'You probably think it's some kind of toothpaste.'

'So what started World War Three?' Dad asks.

'John wants us all to speak French,' says Gary.

He makes a gargling sound in the back of his throat – his attempt at a French accent. It sounds more like somebody swallowing snails.

'Let me get this right,' says Dad. 'You're arguing about linguistics?'

'What we're arguing about,' I say, 'what we're arguing about—'

What *are* we arguing about?

'Oh, he just gets on my nerves.'

I throw the door open and walk down the garden. Quite how I don't know, but I've lost this argument, whatever it was about. Dad joins me a moment later.

'So what was that really about?' he asks.

Maybe it's time to come clean. Not completely, you understand, but clean enough to point Dad in the right direction.

'Look, if I tell you something, promise you won't go after Gary screaming blue murder?'

Dad folds his arms. It's no deal.

'Promise or I say nothing.'

'All right, I promise.'

The tale I tell is a masterpiece, if I say so myself. I leave out most of the big stuff, but tell Dad just enough to set his worry warts tingling. Most of it boils down to this: Adrian still isn't out of the picture.

'Don't say anything, Dad. Please.'

Dad glances up at Gary's room. I haven't told him anything new, but I've blown a hole through his attempt at self-delusion.

'No, my lips are sealed. But I'm going to keep an eye on him.'

Which is all I want: for him to be a proper dad, to be strong, to have the answers.

All the answers.

'What were you telling Dad about?' Gary asks later.

I jump. I didn't hear him coming.

'My exams.'

'Nobody asks about mine,' says Gary.

'You mean you've got some?' I gasp.

'Of course I have, same as everybody else. That's right, my snobby brother, even at Lobotomy High.'

I see his point. Even if anybody does bother to ask Gary how he's doing at school, it's only for show. They're just going through the motions. For a success story they come to me. It's a Me Brainbox, Him Thicko thing.

'You never revise,' I say.

'So? We do it in school.'

'You still have to go over it at home,' I say. 'It won't stick otherwise.'

I'm pointing at my forehead.

'It'd take some pretty powerful glue to make anything stick in here,' says Gary.

I don't believe it. He's got me feeling sorry for him again. I ask you, he has run-ins with the law, slithers round the house like something from the Land of the Living Dead and still he comes up smelling of roses. It could be he was born with some kind of weird charm.

Or it could be because he's my brother.

That evening, I'm up at Yvette's house. I'm indoors this time. We're meant to be revising but I don't think Mrs Tomlinson is under the illusion we're learning much.

'I'm a great believer in R and R,' she says.

That's Rest and something. What is the other R for?

'I used to have friends round when I was revising,' Mrs T says. 'It stopped me getting over-anxious.'

Yvette and I sit at the table with our books spread in front of us. We're meant to be testing each other. Mostly we smile. Once, when my smile drops, she asks if I'm all right.

'Have you got something on your mind, John?'

'It shows, huh?'

'Yes, so what is it?'

'Same as usual. Dad's got his girlfriend round so Gary is playing Superbrat. Maybe I should have hung round to referee.'

'Do you want to go?'

I take her hand.

'No, not yet.'

When I get home the problem hasn't gone away but Gary has. Dad is on his way out.

'Where are you off?'

'I'm going looking for our Gary,' says Dad. 'He's just done a runner.'

'How come?'

'He was being horrible to Rose,' Dad explains. 'We had a flaming row.'

'So where is he now?'

Dad gives a defeated shrug.

'I've no idea.'

Rose comes up behind Dad.

'You must think we're a strange lot,' I say.

'No,' she says. 'Just a family. I've got two boys myself.'

I can't believe I'm thinking this, but she seems OK. She'll never take Mum's place, but I think I could get used to her being around. Dad isn't thinking about any of that stuff. He's worried sick about Gary.

'So he flipped?' I say.

'Completely,' said Dad. 'It's the worst I've seen him.'

Weird as this may sound, I end up staying with Rose while Dad looks for Gary. It isn't long before the situation starts to get to me. I just don't know what to say to her.

'Tell Dad I've gone looking for Gary, too,' I tell her.

'I'm not sure you should,' she says.

I take no notice. She's not my mum.

I've been gone an hour so I pull out my mobile. I check in with Dad.

'Why aren't you at home?' he asks.

'I got fed up waiting. Look, I've an idea where Gary might be. Mick mentioned it once. I'm going over there now.'

'John,' Dad says, 'that might not be such a good idea.'

'How's that?'

'I've been on to Tony Connolly's dad. You know he had a fight with Adrian?'

I don't like the way this is leading.

'Yes.'

'Adrian pulled a knife on him. Good job Tony's dad is an ex-para. He disarmed the little sod, but you can bet he's got himself another one by now.'

'I'll be all right,' I say.

I'm not sure how I know that.

'John,' Dad tells me, 'go home. That's an order.'

At that very moment I spot the blue Fiesta. Without another word I hang up.

The Fiesta is parked on waste ground off Stopgate Lane. I stop, unsure what to do next. Adrian is at the wheel. Gary and Tony are outside the car, leaning against the bonnet.

'Gary!' I shout.

His head snaps round.

'What are you doing here?'

'Looking for you.'

'Dad sent you, I bet.'

'No, in fact he ordered me to stay away. I wanted to come.'

I glance at Adrian and Tony. They don't look too friendly. I'm wondering whether to say something when Adrian steps out of the car.

'Hey you,' he says. 'Grass boy. I hear you blew the boys up to the coppers?'

He must mean that night down County Road.

'I didn't grass on anybody,' I protest. 'All I was doing was warning Gary that—'

I don't get to finish. Adrian takes hold of my shirt collar and twists it until it hurts.

'Listen you, I don't like people grassing up my boys. You keep your nose out of our business. Got that?'

The moment he touches me, my skin starts crawling. My legs have turned to water but I manage a protest.

'Get your hands off me!'

Adrian's eyes narrow. He's loving every minute of this. I can smell the aggression. Violence excites him.

'So make me.'

Gary's feeling uncomfortable.

'Come on, Ade, no need for this.'

'Whose side are you on, Gaz?' says Adrian.

'Nobody's,' says Gary.

In that moment, I've learned something about Gary. He's trying to act big but he's as scared of Adrian as I am.

'I just think,' Gary says, 'if John says he was warning me about some woman with a mobile, then we should believe him.'

'Because he's your brother, right?'

'I suppose so, yeah.'

'Aw, brotherly love, isn't that touching?'

Tony laughs, though it comes out a bit forced. It's obvious Adrian rules the lot of them by fear.

'Gary,' Adrian says, 'from now on I'm your family.'

'But you're going to let him go?'

Adrian gives a humourless smile.

'Is that what you want?'

Adrian responds by swinging me off balance so I end up sprawling on the ground.

'Clear off,' he orders. 'Before I change my mind.'

Gary looks relieved. I spoil the moment.

'Gary,' I say, brushing the grit off my hands, 'forget this moron.'

Sometimes fear isn't enough to keep your mouth shut. I know Adrian can hurt me, but I can't just give in. I've got to get through to Gary.

'Just come home with me.'

'No way!'

I take a step in his direction.

'Gary, just come away, will you?'

I point at the blue Fiesta.

'I bet this is nicked.'

Their faces change. It is, too!

'Don't you ever learn?'

I try dragging Gary away physically. Adrian seems to find it funny. We're still struggling by the factory units when a police car pulls into view.

'Get down!' I bark, shoving Gary's head down. 'If we stay where we are they can't see us.'

Gary fights me for a moment or two then does as he's told. The police car is approaching the Fiesta. Adrian is on the move.

'Lunatic,' I say when it becomes obvious he's going to try to get away.

Adrian and Tony are already in the car. Sean has turned up from somewhere and dives in the back. With one of the doors still swinging open the Fiesta burns rubber and heads straight for the police car. At the last possible moment it swerves away. Within seconds the police car's light is flashing and the siren is blaring. The chase is on. Adrian takes the first corner at high speed and turns right. He's heading for the East Lancs.

'So that's your idea of fun,' I say.

Even Gary is looking shaken.

'No,' he says.

'So you don't get a thrill from it, a buzz?'

His face is closed against me.

'No.'

'I don't believe you.'

Gary's eyes meet mine.

'You want to know what it is? I'll tell you John. With my mates, I've got a family.'

'We're your family, me and Dad!'

'Really?'

'What's that supposed to mean?'

'Mum loved me for me. All she saw was me, Gary. You know what you and Dad see? Just this loser, this waster. I'm no good at school, no good with people. I'm no good, full stop.'

I realise this could be the most he's said to me in one go for weeks.

'We've never said that,' I protest weakly.

'It's the way you think,' he replies.

He puts his face close to mine.

'Tell me you're not thinking that way now.'

'Gary—'

'See, you can't!'

I give Dad a call to put his mind at rest.

'Thank God you're OK,' he says.

'We'll be home in five minutes,' I tell him.

But no sooner have I pocketed my mobile than a figure steps out in front of me. Gooseflesh spreads across my skin. It's Adrian.

'Did you have something to do with that?' he asks.

My heart kicks in my chest. He's got me down as a grass, and I know what happens to kids that squeal. I manage to stammer out a reply.

'The police? Of course not.'

'Don't you think it was a bit of a coincidence?' he asks.

Gary is fidgety. Frightened glances flash between us.

'Say, Ady,' he says, trying to distract Adrian. 'What happened to the others?'

Adrian's stare slides away from me, just for a moment.

'We left the car. We had to split up to lose the coppers.'

His eyes fix me again, pinning me to the spot.

'So you got away?' Gary says.

Adrian nods absent-mindedly. His eyes haven't left my face. He takes a step forward and stabs two fingers into my chest.

'So why'd you do it, Mastermind?'

The tone of his voice chills me to the marrow of my bones. Nothing either Gary or I can do is going to throw him off the scent.

'I beg your pardon?'

His face is right up against mine. Sweat starts out from every pore in my body.

'Why'd you tip off the coppers?'

Gary is squirming.

'Ady, he never!'

Adrian throws a hand out.

'Shut it, Gaz. Once is coincidence. Twice?'

He lets the thought hang for a moment.

'Well, we know what that means, don't we?'

'Look,' I say, 'you've got to believe me. I didn't call the police.'

Adrian roars his contempt in my face.

'Liar!'

I try to push past.

'You're just being stupid.'

154

I wince. Wrong word. I can feel Adrian right up close. He seems to blot out everything else. His voice creeps right under my skin.

'Nobody calls me stupid.'

Something flashes. Gary shouts a warning.

'John, he's got a knife!'

Instinctively, I raise my arm. Something rips. It's my jacket. But it isn't over. Adrian goes for me again. The world tilts, stutters into slow motion. I'm paralysed by fear. Then, before I can do anything to defend myself, Gary dives between us. Finally, real time resumes. There's a cry, then a splash of something thick and warm on my face.

It's blood.

The next few minutes pass in snapshots. Slow motion snaps into a strobing sequence of stills. There's me kneeling down to help Gary, pressing my hands to his stomach, watching in horror as the blood pumps over his shirt.

What do I do?

What the hell do I do?

I'm shoving bits of shirt at the hole, trying to stop the blood coming.

Gary is screaming. It seems to go on forever before I finally make sense of what he's saying, 'Get Dad.'

Suddenly, he isn't hard. He isn't the lad who's been making my life a misery. He's just a scared kid and he needs me. It's as if everything has suddenly come into focus. For both of us. We're brothers. Life's dealt us a lousy hand. Big deal. We've got to get on with it. Right now, we'll give anything for another minute of Gary's life. We've lost Mum. We can't lose anyone else.

Then I'm punching the emergency number with one bloodstained finger. Minutes later – it seems like hours – the police and an ambulance are on the scene. Lights are flashing, gashing the night wide open. There's a stretcher. The questions start.

At long last, with the paramedics telling me they'll do what they can for Gary, it's time for the hardest phone call I've ever made, from inside the ambulance, telling Dad we're on our way to hospital.

17

'That's it then,' says Adam four days later. He ritually peels off his school tie.

'Science, the last exam.'

Olivia is holding court outside the hall, double-checking her answers with the Paradise Set.

'I heard about your Gary,' she sneers. 'Nice company he's been keeping.'

I brush past. Then, from somewhere, I discover a reply laced with venom.

'Drop dead, Olivia.'

I hear her shocked voice following me down the corridor.

'Well, really!'

I spin round.

'Yes, *really*! You know what you are, Olivia?'

Suddenly, I can't wait to tell her.

'You're a spoiled, stuck-up Barbie doll with candyfloss for brains.'

Which is a pretty odd thing to say to somebody who is heading for ten A stars! But heck, I know what I mean. She can be as drop-dead gorgeous and clever as she wants. If it came down to feelings she would be ungraded, simple as that.

'I suppose you think fighting with knives is so *cool*,' she retorts, making inverted commas with her fingers.

I hate people who do that.

'Gary wasn't fighting,' I yell. 'He was attacked. He got stabbed.'

'Well, if you must keep the wrong kind of company –'

By now I'm trembling with fury. Her voice trails off.

'You know what,' I interrupt, my skin burning with rage and shame, 'you're not fit to kiss our Gary's feet.'

I never thought I'd hear myself saying *that*. I mean, you should see the state of Gary's feet. I march away before I say something I'll regret. Kedra is there and I don't want to mess things up for Adam.

'Congratulations,' says Adam when he catches up with me a few minutes later. 'Very professional hatchet-job on Olivia.'

'Thanks. I hope I didn't upset Kedra.'

'No, she thought it was funny. She liked the bit about the Barbie doll. I never expected you to stand up for Gary like that. You've said a lot worse about him yourself since last Friday.'

'I'm allowed to. I'm his brother.'

'How is he, by the way?'

'Fine. He got a few stitches, that's all. He's enjoying all the attention. He's talking about having a tattoo round the scar when he's older.'

'Your dad will love that!'

'Yes, he gave one of his over-my-dead-body speeches.'

'I'll bet. What did he have to say about the attack?'

'He was quite good about it, really. It's like the whole thing has shocked him into getting a grip. He let us talk. For the first time in months, he actually listened to us. We just sat talking for hours.'

'So has Gary learned his lesson?'

'I think we all have. It's a new start. The way I see it with Gary, it's not like he's going to turn into an angel over-night, but I think he's finally rumbled Adrian. We bumped into Sean yesterday. Gary just blanked him.'

'That's something,' says Adam.

'Yes, that's something.'

I take Yvette out for a pizza.

'How'd it go?' she asks.

'It went.'

Suddenly, everybody wants to talk. Most people are just being nosy about the stabbing. Adam and Yvette are the only ones I really open up to. I tell Yvette about my brush with Olivia. Her eyes light up.

'Barbie doll? You really called her that?'

'Yes. I slew the fearsome Bellman with my razor-sharp tongue.'

I might not have been quite so brave if she'd still been going out with Paul Martindale.

'Are you still coming tomorrow?' I ask.

'Yes, I'm really looking forward to it. Doesn't Gary know yet?'

'He hasn't got a clue.'

'I think the whole thing is really sweet.'

'Yes,' I say, reaching for her hand. 'I'm a sweet guy.'

I get a surprise when I get home. Gary and Mick are sitting in the kitchen talking.

'You haven't been round in a while,' I say to Mick.

'I haven't been invited in a while,' he replies.

It was Gary's first day back in school today.

'Did everybody ask you about the stabbing?' I ask him.

'Yeah, I was a real celebrity.'

'I should have let Adrian chop your head off,' I say. 'Then you'd have been really famous.'

'Not funny,' says Gary. 'I can still see that knife coming at me.'

He gives a shudder. He isn't faking it.

'Heard anything about Adrian?' I ask.

'I saw Tony in school,' says Mick.

'You mean you're on speaking terms!'

'Tony's all right,' says Gary. 'A bit dumb, that's all.'

He sees the way I'm looking at him.

'Yes, I know, same as me. You don't have to rub it in all the time.'

'So what's the rumour about Adrian?'

'He's got plenty of previous. He's going away for this.'

Gary looks me in the eye. We don't need to speak.

Dad gets home about half past six.

'Do me a favour, John, lad,' he says. 'Run to the chippy.'

He tosses me a tenner.

'I need something quick. I'm seeing Rose tonight.'

I catch Gary's eye. He keeps quiet – he's got to after Friday – but he still doesn't like it. Rose's name is like a red rag to this particular bull. Some things you don't sort out by talking. I'm starting to wonder if he'll ever come round. Let's face it, I'm still not sure how *I* feel.

'This is getting serious, isn't it?'

Dad nods. All the time I'm at the chippy, I'm worrying whether a row has erupted while I'm away. As it happens, it's all very civilised when I get back.

'Tomorrow night?' Gary is asking. 'What are we doing tomorrow night?'

'Not telling,' says Dad.

'What's the big secret?'

'Wait and see.'

Gary turns to me.

'What's happening?'

'Not telling.'

Gary looks at the calendar. Mum's birthday is still ringed from months ago.

'We can't go out. Not tomorrow. You do realise what day it is?'

Dad settles for a one-word answer, 'Yes.'

'Then we should stay home. It won't feel right going out, not on Mum's birthday.'

He's pleading.

'We can't just forget.'

Dad smiles.

'We won't.'

I'm dying to spill the beans, but Dad warns me off with a glance. Gary hovers on the edge of a tantrum then goes to his room.

Just how much we haven't forgotten, Gary discovers at eight o'clock Saturday night: there are getting on for a hundred people in the function room at Orrell Park Ballroom.

'What is this?' he asks as we climb the stairs.

Getting him here has been murder. He has been getting moodier and moodier all evening. With every resentful look, he has been accusing us of forgetting Mum. But when he follows me into the room his expression changes. He looks shaken. At the front there is a huge picture of Mum, taken on holiday in Talacre. Either side of the photo are two equally extravagant bouquets, red roses.

'We didn't forget,' says Dad.

Gary just stares.

'Quiet, aren't you?' I say.

He's on the verge of tears.

'I don't want to make an idiot of myself,' he says.

'You've done that already,' I reply. 'Tonight we celebrate Mum's life. You're allowed to cry if you want.'

I ruffle his hair.

'Get in touch with your feminine side.'

'John,' Gary says, 'you don't half talk some rubbish.'

Ten minutes later I'm showing Yvette off to the relatives.

'So this is your young lady,' says Grandad Ferguson.

The old guy is very formal. He wears a suit on Sunday,

holds the door open for women and calls them ladies. I ought to find it naff, but there's something very straight and decent about it all. Maybe what I see is a generation who knew where they were going.

'Yvette, meet my grandad.'

Yvette does her half-smile, the braces-concealer. Grandad whispers in her ear. When he's gone I ask what he said.

'That I've got a lovely smile,' Yvette tells me. 'And that I shouldn't hide it.'

The old charmer! Yvette gives my arm a squeeze.

'I like your grandad. Come to think of it, I like your whole family.'

'What, even Gary?'

'Gary's sweet.'

Gary *sweet!* So, what does sugar taste like on your planet, Yvette?

'It doesn't bother you, what happened?' I ask.

Yvette shakes her head.

'Mum was a bit worried. About you more than anything. But no, it doesn't bother me.'

I put my arm round her.

'Do you know how nice you are?'

'Mm, pretty much.'

We laugh. Just then, Grandad Cain flashes the lights and everybody looks in his direction.

'We'd like to thank you for coming, ladies and gentlemen,' he says. 'We're here to celebrate a very special lady. Raise your glasses everyone, to my daughter-in-law, Lisa Cain.'

After the toast, Grandad clears his throat and continues.

'We're all here because Lisa touched every one of our lives, one way or another.'

He introduces Mum's best friend Marie. She says a few words.

'How are you, Gary?' I ask. 'Holding up?'

'Yes, I'm going to make it.'

'I bet you a fiver you're blubbing before the evening is out.'

'Get stuffed!'

'So put your money where your mouth is.'

Gary grins.

'Done.'

Dad speaks next. He keeps it short and gruff. He's closer to tears than Gary is. All the while he's stumbling through his speech his eyes keep darting over to us. He knows we came pretty close to the edge. Tonight's about being a family, making us work and finding our way again after Mum.

Then it's Grandad Ferguson.

'Lisa was my daughter,' he says, 'and I just can't believe she's gone.'

His eyes rove round the room. You could hear a pin drop.

'The reason I can't believe it is simple: she hasn't gone at all.'

He touches his temple.

'She's in here, you see: the baby I held in my arms; the little girl who was always wanting to run messages; the young woman who gave me two fine grandsons.'

I look at Gary.

Going—

'You know what else,' says Grandad, catching Gary's eye. 'Here in my head there's light and dark, dreams and nightmares. Parents are as good as the children they raise. So how did our Lisa do?'

Gary looks down at his shoes.

'When I was a young fellow,' Grandad continues, 'growing up was easy. You had a few fist fights, learned a trade, raised a family. Maybe you had to fight a war along the way.'

He scratches his head and grins.

'Maybe it wasn't that easy.'

There is a ripple of laughter.

'It was tough, really tough sometimes. But, believe me, compared to today it was simple.'

He gives us a look. He obviously knows a lot more than he's been letting on. Did Dad let something slip? I can't see it. More likely, it's down to my uncle Graham. He's a copper. He must have picked something up on the grapevine.

'When I look at John and Gary, I know I wouldn't swap places with them. It isn't easy to see your way ahead these days. The world youngsters are growing up in, they have to make the rules up as they go along. I'm starting to realise how hard that is.'

Gary's eyelids are batting furiously.

. . . going . . .

'Young lads can fly pretty close to the flame but I know if Lisa were watching tonight she'd know that her sons are growing up into fine young men. You did all right, Lisa love.'

Next to me, Gary is crying.

. . . gone!

Grandad finishes his speech. Somebody puts on Mum's favourite songs, *The Story of the Blues* followed by *Heart as Big as Liverpool*. This is classic Liverpool, hard, loud and sentimental. There isn't a dry eye in the house.

'Gary,' I whisper, 'you owe me a fiver.'

It's a while later, Yvette draws my attention to something.

'Why isn't Rose here?'

'I don't know. Maybe she would feel a bit uncomfortable.'

'There's no reason she shouldn't be here now though,' says Yvette. 'I bet your dad would love her to come.'

I give Yvette a peck on the cheek.

'Hang on,' I say. 'I've something to do.'

I find Gary wolfing the sausage rolls.

'Gaz,' I say, 'I think you owe Dad one.'

'Yes,' Gary replies. 'Sounds about right.'

'So I've got a suggestion.'

I hand him my mobile.

'What's this for?'

'To phone Rose.'

'You're joking!'

'Dad loved Mum. He always will. That's what tonight's about.'

'So you're telling me you want me to phone his new squeeze?'

'Listen, Gary. He's got to start again. We're starting to make lives for ourselves. Why shouldn't Dad? Think about it.'

I leave the phone with him. Her number is scribbled on a beer mat.

'It's your call.'

Yvette and I finish dancing. We find the phone and beer mat on our table.

'Your Gary left them with us,' says Adam.

'When?'

'About a quarter of an hour ago.'

He didn't make the call. I'm disappointed in him. I spot him chatting up our cousin Charlotte's best friend.

'You should have made the call,' I tell him.

'Hello, John,' a woman's voice says. 'What call is that?'

I spin round.

'Rose!'

'Where's your dad?'

I point him out. His face lights up when he sees her.

'There you go, bro,' Gary says. 'I think we're quits.'

*

Next day it's just the three of us: Dad, Gary and I. We are leaning over the rail of the Mersey ferry. We are each holding a red rose. We get some funny looks but who cares?

'To Lisa,' says Dad, throwing his rose onto the waters.

'To Mum,' say Gary and I, following his rose with ours.

'And now,' says Dad, 'to us.'

We watch the sun going down over the river. Night is coming. But the sun will rise again.

Also by Alan Gibbons

THE LEGENDEER TRILOGY
The Shadow of the Minotaur

'Real life' or the death defying adventures of the Greek myths, with their heroes and monsters, daring deeds and narrow escapes - which would you choose?

For Phoenix it's easy. He hates his new home and the new school where he is bullied. He's embarrassed by his computer geek dad. But when he logs on to The Legendeer, the game his dad is working on, he can be a hero. He is Theseus fighting the terrifying Minotaur, or Perseus battling with snake-haired Medusa.

The trouble is The Legendeer is more than just a game. Play it if you dare.

Vampyr Legion

What if there are real worlds where our nightmares live and wait for us?

Phoenix has found one and it's alive. Armies of bloodsucking vampyrs and terrifying werewolves, the creatures of our darkest dreams, are poised to invade our world.

But Phoenix has encountered the creator of *Vampyr Legion*, the evil Gamesmaster, before and knows that this deadly computer game is for real - he must win or never come back.

Warriors of the Raven

The game opens up the gateway between our world and the world of the myths.

The Gamesmaster almost has our world at his mercy. Twice before fourteen-year-old Phoenix has battled against him in *Shadow of the Minotaur* and *Vampyr Legion*, but Warriors of the Raven is the game at its most complex and deadly level. This time, Phoenix enters the arena for the final conflict, set in the world of Norse myth. Join Phoenix in Asgard to fight Loki, the Mischief-maker, the terrifying Valkyries, dragons and fire demons - and hope for victory. Our future depends on him.

Julie and Me . . . and Michael Owen Makes Three

It's been a year of own goals for Terry.

- Man U, the entire focus of his life (what else is there?), lose to arch-enemies Liverpool FC
- he looks like Chris Evans, no pecs
- Mum and Dad split up (just another statistic)
- he falls seriously in love with drop dead gorge-ous Julie. It's bad enough watching Frisky Fitzy (school golden boy) drool all over her, but worse still she's an ardent Liverpool FC supporter.

Life as Terry knows it is about to change in this hilariously funny, sometimes sad, utterly readable modern Romeo and Juliet story.

Julie and Me : Treble Trouble

For one disastrous year Terry has watched Julie, the girl of his dreams, go out with arch rival Frisky Fitz, seen his Mum and Dad's marriage crumble and his beloved Man U go the same way. 2001 has got to be better.

- Will he get to run his hands through the lovely Julie's raven tresses?
- What happens when his new streamlined Mum gets a life?
- Can Man U redeem themselves and do the business in the face of the impossible?

Returning the love - that's what it's all about.

Read the concluding part of *Julie and Me* and all will be revealed.

The Edge

Danny is a boy on the edge. A boy teetering on the brink of no return, living in fear.

Cathy is his mother. She's been broken by fear.

Chris Kane is fear - and they belong to him.

But one day they escape. They're looking for freedom, for the promised land where they can start really living. Instead they find prejudice, and danger of another kind.

Uncompromising and disturbing, but utterly readable, Alan Gibbons' latest novel positively crackles with tension as he writes about a mother and her son desperate to start a new life.

Caught in the Crossfire

'You know what happens to people like you? You get hit in the crossfire.'

Shockwaves sweep the world in the aftermath of 11 September. The Patriotic League barely need an excuse in their fight to get Britain back for the British, but this is chillingly perfect.

Rabia and Tahir are British Muslims, Daz and Jason are out looking for trouble, Mike and Liam are brothers on different sides. None of them will escape unscarred from the terrifying and tragic events which will weave their lives together.

Marking a new dimension in his writing on race, riots and real life, *Caught in the Crossfire* is an unforgettable novel that Alan Gibbons needed to write.

'Gibbons' writing often addresses worrying issues of social justice but never as powerfully as in this novel . . . the writing - short, sharp pieces that take us into the mind of each character - is accessible and compulsive.'

Wendy Cooling, *The Bookseller*